Portlanders

Portlanders

Tom Malone

Denver, Colorado · 2020

Library of Congress Control Number: 2020906826
ISBN-13: 978-1-945236-16-7
ISBN-10: 1-945236-16-7

Printed in the United States of America
First edition, 2020

Published by Thomas R. Malone · Denver, Colorado

For Delaney

"Long live the rose that grew from concrete when no one else ever cared."

— Tupac Shakur

INTRODUCTION

Portland, Oregon: just another big American city. Tall buildings, millions of people, systemic problems, and a vibrant culture. It has an airport, food trucks, and traffic. It houses small business, large corporations, old homes, and new complexes. Sports franchises, universities, and museums. Everything that every major city features.

Yet there's something unique about Portland. Mount Hood towers above the skyline, while the Willamette River flows through its center. Water evaporates from the Pacific Ocean, creating massive clouds that roll over the city, dropping inches of rain before rising over the Cascade Mountains. Surrounded by fertile farmland, lush pine tree forests, and epic landforms that rise from the rivers, Portland's geography inspires awe.

The 45th Parallel nearly runs through Portland, placing the city halfway between the North Pole and the Equator. The Columbia River rushes through steep gorges, forming

Portland's northern border with the state of Washington. As the Willamette River flows through downtown Portland, it meets the Columbia, winding about 100 miles northwest until it collides with the Pacific Ocean. The two water forces crash into each other with violence, with ferocity, making this confluence one of the roughest patches of water in the world.

As with any major city, Portland is a cultural melting pot. Some families have roots dating back to the 1850s. And, of course, it has its share of new transplants. Stuffy business-people. Hippies, artists, baristas, mixologists, and creators. Hispanic, Caucasian, African-American, Asian-American, Pacific Islander. Men, women, and non-binary. Young people. Old folks. Impoverished. Wealthy beyond belief. It's a city of contrast.

Centuries ago, Native American cultures thrived off of Portland's abundance. A group of Chinookan people called the Multnomah utilized the Willamette River's natural resources to develop a complex society that echoed the Pacific Northwest's long history of artwork, community, and respect for the land. The Multnomah used the Willamette Valley's open territories as sustainable hunting grounds.

In November of 1805, Lewis and Clark reached the Pacific Ocean, just 100 miles west of Portland with the help of Native American guides. In their makeshift Fort Clatsop, the team of explorers struggled through the cold wind and rain of the Oregon Coast in the winter. When the weather cleared, they set off for their return journey to the East Coast, where they met with President Thomas Jefferson to recount their adventure.

By the late 1830s, the United States government had opened Oregon Territory to any white settlers who made the arduous journey on the Oregon Trail. Native Americans were forcibly removed from the Portland area by the United States government as war against native cultures increased.

As more white colonizers moved into the port city, massive trees were cleared to make room for homesteads and farms. Trees were cleared at such a fast rate that stumps and lumber lay flat along the Willamette River's banks; travelers nicknamed the city "Stumptown", indicating its haphazard appearance. As the city grew, so did its ports. Workers flooded into the city to work on ships and docks, while timber brought in lumberjacks to the surrounding forests. Some were white settlers from the Midwest and East Coast, while black workers moved from the South to establish a new life away from Jim Crow. Immigrants from Asia came in on Pacific ships. Bridges were constructed across the Willamette River, connecting the West Side to the East Side, and the West Side to North Portland.

Portland grew more and more populated with people looking for opportunity, and the city itself began to take shape. Brick buildings rose along the Willamette River. Tunnels weaved underneath the city, serving as transportation between buildings for legitimate goods and illegal activities. With its 3,000-mile distance from Washington, D.C. and its jumping-off point to trading ports in Asia, Portland became a haven for corruption and debauchery in the early 1900s. Its corrupt police force aided in this underworld activity as Prohibition came and went.

As the United States grew more economically powerful after World War II, Portland became a beacon for industry, with shipyards and docks bringing in more and more people. With increasing economic opportunity and a low cost of living, people continued to move into the city, and then the city itself expanded into the suburbs. Public train systems connected the East Side and West Side, while bike paths promoted an ecofriendly mode of travel throughout the city. Skyscrapers replaced old brick buildings, while revitalization and gentrification changed the city's skyline and demographics.

Portland's story is similar to many major cities throughout the United States. It's comparable to many cities throughout the world, in fact. But there's something special about Portland. It could be the way that nature flows through its urban center. It could be the way the mountain rises in line with the skyscrapers. It could be the way that the old blends with the new.

Then again, it could be the people. The people who shape the city. The people who change the city. The people who move into the city from other places, bringing new ideas and priorities. The people who were born in the city and struggle to keep its roots strong. It's people that determine a city's outcome. A city's character. A city's story.

THE NEW ARRIVAL

Henry threw his backpack over his shoulders and stepped off the train. The brick-covered platform buzzed with people, more people than Henry had ever seen in one place. He tried to merge with the crowd, a technique he had yet to master. As he stepped into the flow of foot traffic, a middle-aged man in a suit bumped his shoulder.

"Watch it, pal," the man said.

"Uh, sorry," Henry replied.

Henry continued to follow the crowd into the terminal. When he stepped through the doors, the terminal's grandeur forced him to look up in awe. He wanted to stop and look around the building, but he did not want to risk looking like a tourist. Every other terminal patron moved through the room with purpose, so Henry figured that he should do the same.

Blend in, he thought.

He exited the voluminous room and walked outside onto the sidewalk. The overcast sky produced just enough light to force a squint. Two police cars sped by the train station. Henry wondered what heinous crime could have prompted such a large show of force.

Anxiety crept over Henry, so he took a drink of water from his bottle and placed it back in his backpack. He looked up at the clock tower above the red-brick terminal to check the time. *Union Station* adorned one side of the tower; on the other side: *Go by Train*.

The clock told Henry that it was nearing dinner time. He raised his hand to hail a taxi, just like he had seen travelers do in the movies. The girl next to him did the same.

Henry noticed her charming beauty. She wore little make-up, yet possessed flawless fair skin. Her wide-brimmed hat flopped over one side of her face, while her auburn hair fell over her shoulder. Her entire aura exemplified every preconceived notion that Henry had about Portland's trendy culture. Henry made eye contact with her; he felt locked in her gaze. His face flushed and he quickly averted his eyes, returning his attention to the avoidant taxis.

Finally, a yellow cab pulled up to the curb, bypassing Henry to approach the girl. She opened the cab door, but paused and turned toward Henry.

"Hey," she shouted. "Want to share a ride?"

Henry felt his face flush again.

"Uh, sure," he said.

As he moved toward the taxi, the girl entered and scooted over to make room for Henry. He sat in the open back seat and stuffed his backpack between his knees, looking out the window to avoid an awkward conversation.

"Where to?" the driver asked.

"Cleary's on 23rd," the girl replied.

The driver pressed the gas pedal and accelerated with purpose. The girl looked to her right, analyzing the strange passenger.

"Where are you headed?" she asked Henry.

"Um, I really don't know," Henry said.

"What do you mean?" she asked.

"I just got into town," he said. "I'll be staying at a hotel for a couple days while I find a place to live."

The girl looked at Henry hesitantly, and then cracked a smile of approval.

"Where'd you come from?" she said. "Wait, let me guess. White guy with a red flannel shirt buttoned all the way to the top, freshly pressed. Slightly painted-stained jeans. A full beard. You must be from Montana."

Henry raised an eyebrow and gawked.

"How'd you know?" he asked.

"Your ball cap says *Montana*," she said.

Henry smiled and started to blush again.

"What brings you to Portland?" she continued.

"I'm just looking to branch out," he said. "I've only ever lived in Montana. I grew up in a small town out there. Went to community college in the same town. Started working in the same town. I knew if I didn't get out now, I never would. I'd be one of those guys who never left, and grew old complaining about the good ol' days, even though I never really had any good ol' days."

The girl nodded with approval.

"Why Portland, then?" she asked.

"It seemed like a place where I could meet some new people," he said. "Portland seems so cool. It's full of creative people who are free to pursue whatever they want. I want to be creative. I don't want to be stuck in some box and work my whole life. I want to make things. Draw, write, think, create. Drink beer and coffee and experiment. And I definitely can't do that back home."

Henry paused and smirked.

"Plus, the train ticket was cheap," he said.

They both laughed. The girl looked at Henry and smiled.

"I'm Jordan," she said, feigning a polite wave. "Welcome to Portland."

"I'm Henry," he said.

Jordan turned toward the window. She liked to watch the buildings while she drove in cars. They seemed to blur together into a real-life piece of urban artwork. She smiled and turned to Henry.

"Hey," she said. "Why don't you come out with my friends and I tonight. We're going to a bar that has a cool vibe."

Henry's eyes widened and his eyebrows rose, but he quickly lowered them to project the nonchalance he had seen in the movies.

"Are you sure?" he said. "I wouldn't want to intrude."

"Of course I'm sure," Jordan said. "All my friends are open to meeting and including new people."

Henry walked nervously next to Jordan as they strolled along 21st Avenue. They came to a crosswalk at Everett Street. Henry stopped to look both ways; Jordan continued walking and dodged traffic without breaking her stride.

"Come on, cautious," she yelled to Henry from the opposite curb.

Henry smiled. He saw a break between cars and sprinted across the street.

"We'll work on your city skills," Jordan said.

As they approached the doorway to the Cleary's Tavern, Henry grabbed the door and let Jordan enter first. Henry's hesitation caused him to lag behind, so Jordan grabbed his hand and pulled him further into the bar. A group of four people waved toward Jordan. She pulled Henry to the table.

"What's up, guys?" Jordan said. "This is Henry. He just came in from Montana."

The group waved and shouted greetings his way. Henry sat across from Jordan and next to a guy with a moustache. But not a grizzled moustache like the old farmers wore in Montana. This moustache was pristine, maybe even waxed and sculpted. He wore glasses, though Henry was certain that the lenses didn't do anything to help his eyesight.

"Welcome to Portland, man," the mustached guy said. "I'm Jonas."

Jonas handed a menu to Henry.

"What are you drinking?" Jonas asked. "Let me buy you a beer."

Henry was hesitant about the friendly gesture. He had read

about the city lifestyle, and about the deceit that can occur. Pickpockets. Crime. Credit card scams. But he decided to test the atmosphere.

"I'll have a beer," Henry said.

"What kind?" Jonas asked, smiling smugly.

"A light beer," Henry said.

The girl next to Jonas gawked at Henry. Her feather earrings seemed to flutter.

"Dude," she said. "We don't drink that stuff here. That's almost sacrilegious."

Jordan smiled at Henry from across the table. Henry returned a nervous smile.

"Then I'll have whatever you're drinking," he said.

"Great choice," Jonas said. "I'm drinking a Writer's Block IPA from the brewery down the road. One of my favorite drinks in the city. They use organic Cascade hops, grown locally, of course. It really brings out the complexities of the region."

"We're still talking about beer, right?" Henry said.

The bar continued to fill with young people. People in their early 20s, early 30s, even late 60s. People with beards, business suits, flannel vests, and cycling shirts. People with tattoos, piercings, and church clothes.

The lights dimmed and the music volume raised slightly, precisely at 7:30. Patrons of Cleary's Tavern took turns at the billiards tables in casual games. Most resulted in the loser buying the next round.

Henry enjoyed his beer slowly. It packed a serious punch, especially compared to the mass-produced light beer he was used to.

"So, what do you do in Portland?" Henry asked Jonas.

"Well," he said, "I moved here last year from Southern California. I work as a barista at a coffee shop in the Pearl."

"What's a barista?" Henry asked.

"I'm a coffee artist," Jonas said. "I handcraft espresso concoctions."

Seems a bit pretentious, Henry thought.

"I also paint," Jonas continued. "I have some of my work in an art gallery on Alberta. You know, North Portland is really up-and-coming."

"I haven't been there yet," Henry said.

"You should come to an art show with us on Saturday," Jonas said.

Jordan watched and slightly enjoyed seeing Henry engage in this conversation.

"I met Jonas at this Indie concert a few months ago," Jordan said. "His girlfriend is my roommate. We live in an apartment just down the street."

"Jordan hasn't barred me from the apartment yet," Jonas said.

She rolled her eyes and laughed facetiously. Then she returned her attention to Henry.

"Jordan, I don't even know what you do in Portland," Henry said.

She smiled and looked down at her plate of tater tots.

"I'm a cook," she said. "I work at this new start-up restaurant on the East Side called Portland Chow. I usually operate our food truck, but we're trying to transition to a brick-and-mortar location too. No one is really doing brick-and-mortar, so we want to be pioneers and lead that charge."

"That sounds fun," Henry said, still processing the terminology Jordan just used.

He fidgeted with a napkin and glanced anxiously around the bar. He saw a blue moon with a face smiling at him. Henry found himself returning the smile, and then refocusing his attention on Jordan.

"Are you from here?" Henry asked. "You seem to know everything about the city."

"No," Jordan said. "I'm from Idaho. I moved here to make a name for myself in the world of food. Nothing in Idaho but potato dishes."

Henry laughed; his family store in Montana acquired all of their potatoes from an Idaho distributor.

"Are the rest of your friends from Portland," Henry asked.

"No, actually none of them are," Jordan said. "They're from all over the country."

Henry nodded his head slowly. He had yet to meet a person who was actually from Portland.

Jordan challenged Henry to a game of billiards. She made a bet with him; the loser buys the next round.

Henry broke, so Jordan shot next. Her first shot knocked a stripe into the corner pocket. She shrugged her shoulders and winked at Henry. He felt an immediate sense of attractive competition. On her next shot, Jordan ricocheted the cue ball of the wall and knocked in another stripe. Then, she aimed to tap the cue ball gracefully against the stripe situated near the side pocket, but her touch was just too soft.

"Watch me work," Henry said.

"Alright there, stud," Jordan said.

Henry's first shot slammed into a solid that was located at the far end of the table. It bounced hard off the wall, slammed into another wall, and found a side pocket. Henry winked at Jordan.

"Lucky shot," she said.

"Hey, I'd rather be lucky than good," he said.

Henry's next shot sent the cue ball bouncing hard off of three consecutive walls without hitting a single ball. Jordan strutted into place to continue her skillful game. Within a minute, she had three stripes in three separate pockets. Eventually, all she saw was the eight ball, and plenty of solids.

"Eight ball, corner pocket," Jordan said. "Better get your money ready for my drink."

"You have to make it first," Henry said.

Jordan lined up her shot, and then looked directly into Henry's eyes. She struck the cue ball and it knocked the eight ball into the assigned corner pocket. Jordan strolled toward Henry and shrugged her shoulders.

"My dad ran a pool hall in Idaho," she said. "I'll have a Writer's Block from the bar."

Jordan walked toward Henry, patted him on the shoulder, and returned to her seat. Henry's jaw dropped. He had never met a woman with such confidence and assertion.

He walked to the bar, which was crowded with people at this point in the night. With a hand raised, he tried to coax the bartender's attention, but his efforts were unsuccessful. Thirsty customers elbowed their way in front of Henry, pushing him further from the bar. Finally, he dodged his way through the crowd until he found his way to the bar top. The bearded bartender nodded at Henry.

"Two Writer's Block IPAs, please," Henry shouted.

The bartender grabbed two pint glasses and filled them meticulously. Henry noticed the tattoos on the bartender's forearms. Pine trees, mountains, a distinct bridge, and the shape of the state of Oregon all fused together into a tattoo that projected real Oregon authenticity.

The bartender grabbed the pint glasses and set them in front of Henry. He gave the bartender his credit card, and the bartender swiped it. As he returned the credit card, Henry noticed a rose weaving through the bartender's tattoo.

"Hey," Henry said, "where are you from?"

The bartender smiled and looked at Henry with an earnest expression.

"California."

THE OLD MAN

Malcolm sat down in a wooden chair on his front porch, like he did every Saturday morning. He cherished the sunny days that July brought to the city. The sun had been up just long enough to produce the perfect combination of morning briskness and summer heat.

Malcolm liked to watch the city wake up. He liked to watch people open their doors and grab the morning paper. He enjoyed waving to neighbors as they walked their dogs down his sidewalk. He loved the way his corner lot faced the green street signs of Mississippi Avenue and Mason Street.

He peeled part of an orange and tossed the rind near the rose bush; it was good for the soil. A food truck sped down the street; the words *Portland Chow* adorned the side of it.

Across the street, a young couple emerged from their front door. Malcolm tipped his cap to them, but the couple did not seem to notice. They looked at their phones and walked quickly down the sidewalk, lost in finding directions to some new, hip restaurant.

I remember when the people in that house used to get their mornin' paper, Malcolm thought. *Now, these young kids just read the news on their phones. No interaction.*

Peeling more rind from his orange, he noticed his hand. More wrinkled than it used to be. More weathered. Less dexterous.

A woman walked down the sidewalk with her terrier. Malcolm tipped his cap to her, but she was engulfed in her phone conversation.

Is common courtesy not the norm anymore? he wondered.

Malcolm removed his hat from his head and fanned his face. He loved his hat: a maroon fedora with a medium brim and a blue band. He bought this hat with his own money a long time ago for his 21st birthday. His brother thought Malcolm was crazy for buying himself a hat for his own birthday, but Malcolm didn't mind. He wanted to look good. More importantly, he wanted to feel good.

His brothers took him to a bar just down the street on Mississippi Avenue. They thought about driving downtown to go cruising, but black people were hassled downtown back then. As a band of black Portlanders, they decided to stick to North Portland like they usually did. It was safer for them to avoid the white neighborhoods. A bar on Mississippi had live jazz music every night; that was the place.

"What a night," he said.

Malcolm peeled another piece from his orange. The jazz bar was still there. Well, the building was, anyway. Now, it served as a trendy coffee shop for hipsters. Four white guys strolled down the sidewalk, probably to sit in that coffee shop and order something fancy. Double macchiatos and artisan croissants. The trendy group had a collection of moustaches, piercings, tattoos, flannel shirts, and beanies.

Oh, how my neighborhood has changed, he thought.

He tipped his hat to the group as they passed. One guy gave Malcolm a head nod.

"Better than nothin'," Malcolm said.

His eyes followed the group as they strolled North on Mississippi.

I remember when this used to be a black neighborhood, he thought. *When this place felt like home. When white people from the West Side wouldn't dream of comin' over here.*

Malcolm had spent his whole life on Mississippi Avenue. He grew up three blocks down the street, and he bought his own house on Mississippi when he turned 19. He had worked hard through high school at an auto shop to earn money, and he was good at saving it, with the exception of his fedora.

He attended the public high school down the block. He earned good grades, especially in math. He ran track, and he ended up coaching at that high school in his twenties as a way to give back to the community that he loved so much.

After high school, Malcolm continued working at the auto shop as a mechanic. He worked his way up and eventually became the manager of the shop. When Old Joe decided to sell his business, he came to Malcolm, who bought it with the money he had saved. He bought the business and all of the equipment inside the old brick building. The catch: he didn't own the *building*. He had to rent.

Just last year, Malcolm sold the shop. He didn't want to sell his business, but he couldn't afford to pay the rent and still make a decent profit.

The building had changed ownership dozens of times since Malcolm began working at the auto shop. Whoever owned it lately decided to jack up the price of rent to match the gaining popularity of the neighborhood.

The Mississippi neighborhood was becoming prime real estate. Hip businesses were buying up all the old brick buildings and refurbishing them to look more worn down. Young white families and rich entrepreneurs continued to buy up houses just to tear them down and build trendy homes and swanky apartment complexes. Families who had been renting their homes in this neighborhood for decades were forced to move as landowners increased rent costs exponentially.

Malcolm's neighborhood was becoming gentrified. All the black families he grew up with had moved away. Most of them moved further East, where housing was cheaper. Some could not afford to pay the rising cost of rent. Some could not turn down the money that these white investors were throwing their way. And, Malcolm knew that some families moved because they didn't feel comfortable with the crowd that continued to move in.

Malcolm owned his house outright; he paid off his final mortgage nearly twenty years ago. He felt lucky that he hadn't decided to rent a home in his young adult life; if he had, he wouldn't be able to afford the ridiculous cost of rent that these greedy landowners were forcing people to pay in this neighborhood today.

He also recognized that he had an obligation to hold out. He represented all of the original families from this neighborhood. The ones who built it. The ones who couldn't stay and continue to shape its future. Every two months or so, a new real estate investor would come knocking on his door and offer him an outrageous amount of money to sell his house. Malcolm knew he could profit heavily from his original investment, but he always refused to sell.

"I feel like I'm the last black man left on this block," he told his wife, who joined him on the front porch. "Even our boys have moved out of the city."

She smiled and gazed at the street signs.

"We've been through it all here, Malcolm," she said.

Malcolm remembered when Dr. Martin Luther King, Jr. was assassinated. Businesses throughout the neighborhood went up in flames as Malcolm's black community showed their outrage. Even Malcolm took to the streets to show his frustration.

In the 1980s, Malcolm remembered feeling another sense of anger at the direction his neighborhood was moving; it became gang territory. He understood the cause, but he despised the effect. With government systems designed to keep black Americans oppressed and in poverty, community members had enough. They looked to each other for protection against oppressors. But, eventually, the gangs began to target each other instead of the real enemy: systemic injustice.

For a few years, he felt like a prisoner in his own house.

For a few years, walking down his own street at night became a dance with death. Malcolm stuck to wearing neutral colors in the gangland that his community had become.

Those were dangerous times.

It was during this era that a new sound began to ring out in the streets. A bass-heavy, funk-fueled poetry that echoed from car stereos and front porches. This new sound called hip-hop began to persuade the younger members of his community to rise up and take their neighborhood back.

Malcolm remembered how his community rallied to clean up the neighborhood. Malcolm became a leading force in the neighborhood's anti-gang movement. He helped to start a community food bank that would help struggling families so they did not have to turn to gangs for supplies. He volunteered at an organization that helped young black men acquire jobs immediately after graduating from high school. He re-enlisted as a volunteer coach for the local youth league, and he brought his own sons along as coaches too.

After a few years of hard work, Malcolm began to see the results. Families emerged from their homes at night to sit on their porches, or to take a walk with their children, or play games in the street. Young kids walked their dogs at dusk, and rode their bikes along the sidewalks. Mississippi resurrected itself. Once again, it was the neighborhood that Malcolm knew.

Now, he saw his neighborhood changing again. This time, it was not dangerous gangs that made him feel uncomfortable. It was a new culture. A culture of pretentiousness. Values of greed, of ignorance, of pompousness. *Affluenza*, as he had heard it described.

Malcolm peeled another slice off his orange and offered it to his wife. She took the offering and smiled softly to show her appreciation.

Mississippi was different from the rest of Portland's old neighborhoods. It carried with it a history that showed itself through the buildings and the houses. Through the business and the street signs. But the neighborhood also possessed a culture that Portland's other neighborhoods lacked. It emitted a certain vibrancy from the people that built it. From the people that inhabited the homes and businesses. From the people that lived there because that was the only place they were allowed to live. This vibrant culture emerged from a desperation that transformed into pride.

It was this sense of pride that Malcolm was afraid to lose. Not the pride in himself, but the collective pride. The pride that his neighborhood, his culture, and his people had built and rebuilt over generations. A pride that the invading culture could not recognize.

As Malcolm finished his last orange slice, a car pulled up to the curb in front of his house. The car was new; it still glowed with a waxy shine. A man stepped out and closed the car door. He stood on the sidewalk and pulled a pair of sunglasses from his pocket. He looked around at the old Mississippi houses and smiled before putting on his sunglasses.

Malcolm watched the man as he stood on the sidewalk. His pretentious attitude exuded from his stance. He wore a pastel-colored button-up shirt tucked into his tan suit pants.

His slicked-back hair was combed without a flaw.

The invaders are here, Malcolm thought.

The man walked toward Malcolm's house. His dress shoes click-clacked slowly as he approached the front lawn and made his way to the base of the front porch. The man removed his sunglasses and looked at Malcolm with contemptuous eyes. Malcolm raised an eyebrow and stared directly at the man.

"Can I help you?" Malcolm said, knowing exactly what this man wanted.

The man feigned a friendly smile.

"My name is Simon Coronado," the man said. "I'm a real estate agent in the area."

Malcolm's wife stepped to the porch column and crossed her arms.

"I've sold eight houses on this street in the last eight months," Simon continued. "I want to talk to you about selling yours."

Malcolm remained seated and continued to make direct eye contact with the real estate agent, who shifted his weight nervously from one foot to the other.

"You know," he continued, "in this hot market, it's really time to sell. I sold a house last month that went for ten percent over asking price."

Simon paused and waited for Malcolm's shocked expression, but his eyes never wavered.

"I'm sure you've thought about selling," Simon said. "For a guy like you, now is the time to sell. You could really benefit from the popularity of this neighborhood."

Malcolm stood from his chair and placed himself next to his wife. He crossed his arms and stared directly at Simon.

"A guy like me?" Malcolm said. "What do you know about a guy like me?"

Simon smiled. He was already formulating his next line. This was the line he had used eight times this year to convince aging families in urban neighborhoods to sell their houses for astronomical prices. This was the line that allowed him to buy a new car, vacations to the islands, and rental properties all over North Portland. This was the line that hooked every homeowner like Malcolm.

"I know that a guy like you just wants to do what's best for his family," Simon said. "I can tell that you're a *provider*. And now is the time to provide."

Simon smirked, knowing he had won the battle. Now, he wanted to expedite the process.

"Think about the future," Simon continued. "Think about how you want your grandchildren to grow up."

Malcolm returned the smirk. He rubbed his hands together. He felt the weathered, worked skin as he circled his wedding ring. He tipped the brim of his hat up so that this real estate agent could see his face clearly.

"You're right, sir," Malcolm said. "I am a man who wants to provide for my family. That's exactly what I've done, and that's what I'll continue to do. I provided my family with an income, with food on the table, with access to education. I provided my family with time, love, and care. This neighborhood has provided us with those same elements."

Simon's lips curled into a smirk; he was waiting for

Malcolm to admit defeat. He knew it was coming.

"You talk about the future I want for my grandchildren," Malcolm continued. "In order to see the future, you have to know the past. You don't know anything about this neighborhood, about its people, about its history. You don't know anything about its beauty, its struggle, its passion. You don't respect this neighborhood, yet you want to shape its future."

Malcolm paused to gauge Simon's reception of the phrase. Since he seemed indifferent, Malcolm continued.

"And you have the nerve to talk about my grandchildren," he said. "You know what I want for my grandchildren? I want this neighborhood to shape their future like it has shaped my past. I want them to experience the love and vibrant life that this neighborhood provides."

Simon opened his mouth to counter Malcolm's verbal assault, but he struggled to formulate a logical reply.

"And before you waste any more of my precious time with my wife on this lovely Saturday morning," Malcolm said, "I'm going to ask you to step off my lawn, get back in your car, and go find another neighborhood to uproot."

Without turning his back, Malcolm returned to his seat. Simon plastered a fake smile, the smile of a man who knew he had been defeated. A man who knew that he would never feel the ethical repercussions of his drive for money and power. Malcolm smiled back, knowing that he would continue to resist, hoping that he was not the only one left.

THE SINGLE MOTHER

Lucy looked in the mirror as she finished adjusting her makeup. Her dark eyes contrasted against her seemingly flawless white skin, which had been lightened with an old shade of foundation. Her perfectly tailored eyebrows balanced above subtle green eyeshadow, which matched her emerald necklace. Red lipstick gave her face a certain elegance. She fine-tuned the liner around her lips; nothing could be out of place tonight. After all, her ex-husband would be there.

After wiping a single eyelash away from her nose, Lucy stepped into her walk-in closet to look at herself in the full body mirror. She swayed from left to right, and her green dress flowed in rhythm.

Carefully, she walked down her wooden staircase, holding the handrail to steady herself on her impossibly thin heels. She stepped into the kitchen and found her three children sitting around the granite kitchen island. Lucy stood in the doorway and waited for her children to look up, but they remained focused on their devices instead.

Lewis, her 15-year-old son, texted wildly on his phone. He was waiting for an invitation from his girlfriend to attend the ball at her father's country club. All of the most popular kids in Lewis' school would be there; most families at the school belong to the illustrious establishment, which cemented a family's status in the Portland elite. Lewis knew his mother would never have the means to belong, but that would not stop him from making it through the gates.

Lucy's 13-year-old daughter sat next to Lewis. She was watching a video from a popular fashion magazine that described different ways to wear hair that would make boys do a double take. As she watched, she half-tried the various hairstyles that the video suggested. She looked at her reflection on her phone screen and contorted her lips to imitate the expressions of the models in the video.

Jamie, the 9-year-old, stared intently at his tablet. His pointer finger tapped rapidly. He was enveloped in a video game. Jamie tapped faster; his eyes widened. He was immune to anything outside the parameters of the screen.

The massive flat screen television flashed a local news story about gentrification in North Portland. The reporter was standing on Mississippi Avenue, a side of the city that Lucy rarely saw.

Lucy could not wait any longer for her children to acknowledge her presence. She approached the kitchen island and stood against the countertop.

"Well, kids," she said, "I'm leaving."

The three children remained engulfed in their devices.

"Look at me please," Lucy said.

Lewis lifted his head from his phone screen and looked at his mother in annoyance.

"Lewis, you're in charge tonight," Lucy continued. "There's dinner in the fridge. Make sure your brother is in bed before 9:30. And spend some time with each other instead of on your screens, please."

"Fine, Mom," Lewis said.

"The gala ends around ten, and I'll be home after that," Lucy said. "Jamie. Ellen. Be good for your brother."

Lucy touched her daughter's shoulder, turned, and left the kitchen. She walked through the dining room and gathered her purse from the entryway table.

"Bye, kids," she shouted. Her voice echoed through the house's vaulted ceilings.

As Lucy opened the front door, she turned to look at the staircase. The ornate wooden handles spiraled along the curvature of the falling steps. She remembered the first time that she saw the staircase. Her then-husband, Geoffrey, had just purchased the house. Lucy and Geoffrey had been married for six months, and she was still learning how to interact in his elevated social circle. Lucy did not come from money, but Geoffrey was born and raised in the West Hills. His parents were prominent figures among Portland's social elite, and Geoffrey had stepped into their role. His position as a downtown banking executive legitimized his social clout. Lucy knew that she did not belong in Geoffrey's world, and his parents subtly reminded her of it frequently. Lucy hated the whispers that she heard early in her marriage; socialite women called her a trophy wife. Geoffrey was fifteen years older, but the petty gossip was unnecessary.

As she stood in her doorway, she could not help but feel a sense of sadness. It had been two years since the divorce. She won custody rights to the kids, and she won the mansion in the West Hills. But, without the social security of Geoffrey, Lucy knew she would never be fully accepted into Portland's upper class.

She closed the door behind her, walked across the driveway, and unlocked her luxury SUV. The car pulled down the long, tree-lined driveway and accelerated onto the winding road through the forest. With sparse streetlights and dense trees, the road was difficult to see in twilight.

The SUV sped deeper into the forest before emerging onto a well-lit road. As she approached the Portland Club, Lucy felt a sudden shortness of breath. Stopped at a red light, she rolled down her window and breathed slowly. The splashes of light rain felt refreshing and produced a small sense of calm. She rolled up the window and pulled into the country club parking lot.

A valet approached the car and opened the door. He helped Lucy down from the car, not out of necessity, but out of useless formality. As the SUV pulled away, Lucy was left alone. She hesitated to walk into the gala, but the light rain felt cold against her bare shoulders, so she stepped through the doorway.

A doorman took Lucy's coat and purse, while a server

offered her a glass of wine, which she accepted without hesitation. A woman in the ballroom saw Lucy wandering in the country club entryway, so she waved excitedly. Lucy reciprocated with a nervous wave. She felt uncomfortable standing by herself, so she walked over to the woman and her group of friends.

"Lucy, dear," the woman said.

"Hi, Gwen," Lucy said.

"Ladies," Gwen said, "this is Lucy. She often attends galas like these. You may recognize her."

"I don't," a woman said. "Welcome, dear."

Lucy acknowledged the group of three women with a brief smile and nod. They returned the polite gesture, and then continued their conversation.

"Ideally, this fundraiser will net nearly a million for the trust," a woman said.

"With the high-powered men in this room, I have no doubt," another said.

Lucy scanned the room nervously. She had yet to see her ex-husband, but she knew he could be close.

"However," the woman continued, "I am surprised to see some unusual faces here."

"Like who?" Gwen asked.

"Well," the woman said, "Dr. Kapoor is here with his wife from India. They're dressed rather oddly."

Lucy looked around the room in search of the Indian couple, partly to see their outfits, partly to judge this woman's prejudices.

"I'm sure your grandparents are rolling in their graves,"

Gwen said.

The woman threw her head back in laughter.

"Lucy," Gwen said, "her family has been a member of the Portland Club since its foundation in 1914. She's part of the Club's founding families."

Lucy feigned interest, and the woman continued her analysis of the crowd.

"It gets better," the woman said. "When I first arrived, I saw the Coles by the appetizer display. I can't remember ever seeing a black family here. What is this club coming to?"

The group of women laughed. Lucy found herself laughing too. Not in approval for the comment, but out of a need to fit in with the group. She knew that she should say something, but the fear of ostracism was too strong.

"You know", the woman continued, "I always love seeing some of these wealthy men strut into these galas with their new girlfriends."

Lucy shifted nervously from one leg to the other.

"You can tell that these men married for convenience the first time," the woman said, "and then they realized that their money could attract any woman they wanted, so they dropped one and picked up a newer model."

The woman laughed.

"I must have been the newer model," Gwen said.

The women laughed louder. Lucy chuckled politely. She felt herself beginning to perspire.

"It's strange to me that some of these older models who had no previous connection to the Club still seem to hang around, even after their time has expired," the woman said.

"Some of these women aren't even members. But they want to hang on to our coattails by attending these fundraisers. It's all about appearance in our world, I tell you."

Lucy wanted to berate this woman. But she held her tongue, knowing that she needed this woman's approval to maintain a certain level of social status.

"You know that handsome banker?" a woman said.

"The recently divorced man who graciously left the mansion and three children to his wife?" another woman said. "His family has been a part of the Club for decades."

"That's the one. I heard that he's bringing his new girlfriend. You know, that actress from that television show."

"Now that's a new model," Gwen said.

"She must be 25 years old," a woman said. "You can't buy a body like that."

Lucy bit the inside of her cheek. She wanted to cry. She could not stand to listen to this conversation any longer.

"If you'll excuse me, I'm going to find the little girls' room," Lucy said.

Gwen smiled, but her smile began to fade as she realized the impact of her words. A feeling of guilt gripped her.

Lucy sped across the ballroom floor. She dodged through the growing crowd. She needed fresh air. She turned to leave the ballroom through a side door, but then she saw him. And her.

THE MOGUL

Stephen sat in his leather armchair. He set his coffee on the refurbished wood table and stood, raising his arms above his head to stretch. He walked to his window and looked out above the city. As he watched the sunrise, he reveled in his decision to stay home instead of attending the Portland Club's gala last night. *Too many people I don't know who want to pretend we're old pals just so they can snag a donation*, he thought.

His one-bedroom flat covered the entire top floor of a high-rise building in the Pearl District. The open-concept condo provided a panoramic view of the city. The Fremont, Broadway, and Steel Bridges crossed the Willamette River to the east. On clear days, Stephen could even see Mount Hood's iconic peak from his window. He often stood in his window while he drank coffee each morning and watched the sunrise over the mountain and the city. He spent his nights cooking dinner on the other side of his flat. The kitchen's wall of windows gave him an ideal view of the sunset over the West Hills.

When Stephen moved to Portland from Seattle, he bought this condo for the view. And for the location. Stephen knew that he needed to be surrounded by people, so he moved to the center of downtown. There were always people pulsating through this part of the city. But he also selected this flat for its location on the fifteenth floor. His was the only condo on the level. No risk of meeting new neighbors. No need to exchange useless pleasantries with other homeowners. No need to wave out the window to the casual passerby. It was isolation in the middle of the city. A hermitage above the crowd.

Some of his peers did not feel the need to isolate themselves; in fact, many of them loved the spotlight. One of his former business partners bought a basketball team. Another started a high-profile non-profit organization that seemed to grace the cover of national magazines each week. Another even made a run for political office. But not Stephen.

He moved away from the window and walked into the kitchen to refill his coffee cup. As he returned to the window, he passed a framed poster that hung from the wall. This classic rock band poster hung in Stephen's bedroom when he was in high school. Now, it served as a constant reminder of where he came from, a way to remain true to his roots.

Stephen started his software company in his bedroom in high school. As an openly gay 17-year-old boy in Seattle, he was often ridiculed by the popular crowd. As a result, he withdrew and did not have many friends. Instead of going to high school functions, football games, and popularity-contest social events, Stephen spent his free time alone in his room. He built a rudimentary computer from spare parts he scrounged from local businesses, and from there, he developed the original software.

During his freshman year at a college in Seattle, he found solace in the technology department, where he met a few like-minded techies. They helped him continue to develop his software. With the help of friends from the business school, the software was mass-produced and mass-marketed before Stephen's junior year. By the time he turned 21, Stephen was a multi-millionaire.

When he graduated, he moved to downtown Seattle. Stephen and his co-founders bought an old brick building and renovated it; it became the first headquarters for their technology empire.

Stephen met his partner at a basketball game. One of Stephen's co-founders bought a basketball team in Seattle, so Stephen would often attend. Famous celebrities, business leaders, and political figures frequented the suite, which gave Stephen anxiety. Usually, he would grab a plate of food and a drink and move to the front of the box where he could watch the game away from the layered discussions that went on at the bar. One night, a man sat next to him, apparently with the same idea. The man was the brother of a famous actress, but he despised the phony conversations that occurred at these events. Stephen could relate.

Six months later, the man moved into Stephen's mansion on Lake Washington. The law forbade same-sex marriage, but that did not stop Stephen from proposing. They held a ceremony on the lake; no guests, just them. For 18 years, they lived happily on the shores of Lake Washington. They attended business functions, movie premiers, art galas, and fundraisers for international causes. Until the fatal car crash.

Stephen's partner was driving home from the grocery store when a semi-truck ran a red light and smashed the car against a tree. Stephen spiraled. He grieved, but he had no one to grieve with. He became more and more reclusive. He could not show his face at work, so he sold all of his shares in the company's stock. He could not stand to be in his own house; every room reminded him of lost love. He could not even handle entering the city; too many people and too many memories. He needed a change.

He packed only his necessities: a few pieces of memorabilia from his childhood, furniture he had made, and objects to evoke happy memories of his partner. Stephen packed his car and drove. With no plan, he sped south on Interstate 5 until he could no longer feel the haunting memories.

He thought about speeding to San Francisco. After all, San Francisco was the bastion of technology corporations and acceptance of the gay community. But Stephen knew that if he lived in the Bay Area, he would feel pressured to return to the technology field. A major company would seek out Stephen's high profile, and he would be back in the world that he was desperately trying to escape. He thought about driving further south to Palm Springs, another sanctuary city for the gay community, but he could not handle 100-degree weather.

He continued driving through the Washington forest until the trees thinned into a metropolitan area. When he drove into downtown Portland, he felt as if a cloud had lifted. This would be the stop. Spotting the tallest apartment building in the city, he called his agent, who arranged an impromptu viewing of their biggest condo. Stephen bought it outright.

It had been three years since Stephen moved to Portland. He refused to return to Seattle; Portland was home now. The city government continued to pass progressive laws that made Stephen feel welcome. The people welcomed Stephen for who he was, regardless of his money. He knew that when the time was right, he could make new friends that respected him and his lifestyle. But only when the time was right. For now, Stephen was content watching the city from above, drinking coffee, and watching the sunrise.

With his coffee cup empty, Stephen moved away from the widow. He removed his slippers and put on sneakers, along with a light jacket to cut the morning chill. He walked to his elevator and dropped to the ground level. The woman at the front desk quickly closed her magazine and returned to a professionally alert posture.

"Good morning, sir," she said.

"Good morning, Molly," Stephen said, looking at her magazine. "What's new in the celebrity world today?"

Molly blushed.

"Well, the dresses on last night's red carpet were stunning," she said.

"They always are," Stephen said.

He smiled and walked out of the lobby and onto the sidewalk. Stephen loved his morning walk. Rain or shine, he strolled around the city every morning. He loved the atmosphere. Business people and shop owners hustling to work or to a meeting. The city came alive every morning, and even though he played no part in the pulse of the city, simply being there pulled him in.

Stephen walked for a few blocks until he reached his favorite coffee shop. Although he had two cups before leaving his flat, Stephen wanted the cafe experience. It brought him closer to people without having to make useless small talk.

"Good morning," the barista said.

"Good morning," Stephen replied. "I'll have a cappuccino, please."

"Excellent choice," the barista said. "We'll have that out for you in just a minute."

Stephen saw a small table in the corner. He sat against the wall so he could see out into the room and observe. The coffee shop buzzed with life. Some casual table conversations arose from people who had nowhere to be in a hurry, while others sped through the line to acquire their to-go cups before they continued their hustle.

After a half hour of people-watching and reading the newspaper, Stephen left the coffee shop. He walked to his favorite bookstore, Quimby's, a maze of aisles that wound through Portland's underground. A few new titles in the store's entryway caught his eye, but he passed them and moved to the classic fiction section. After selecting a title by Oscar Wilde, Stephen walked toward the bookstore's magazine area. He picked up an issue of a popular business magazine and laughed; one of his co-founders was on the cover, of course.

"I want to be rich like that guy one day," a kid said.

Stephen smiled and looked at the kid.

"You do?" Stephen said. "Why?"

"He bought his own basketball team," the kid said. "He can buy whatever he wants."

"There's more to life than just buying things, kid," Stephen said.

"Not really," the kid said.

"Sure there is," Stephen said. "There's love, happiness, experiences, people."

The kid's face looked puzzled.

"How can you even say that?" the kid said. "You don't even know what it would be like to be super rich."

Stephen smiled.

"I have all the money in the world, kid," Stephen said. "I actually started the company that this guy works for. Take it from me; there's more to life than money. Pursue what makes you happy."

The kid's eyes widened. The impact resonated and grew. Stephen placed the magazine back on the shelf, turned, and walked to another aisle.

THE EAST SIDE KID

Jermaine tapped his pencil eraser on his desk on the side of the classroom. He watched the clock, which seemed to slow down the longer he stared. The teacher stood at the front of the room, where she gave last-minute reminders about the weekend's homework project.

Jermaine looked sideways to Olubowale, who pressed his face against the desktop, covering it with his thin dreadlocks. Jermaine rubbed his own shaved head to keep himself awake. The late spring heat filled the room, making Jermaine feel drowsy. Since the old school building had no air conditioning, the windows were open, which hardly alleviated the stagnant humidity. Jermaine thought about those high-rise buildings he could see across the river. The ones that probably overlooked the whole city. The ones with air conditioning. *What a life*, he thought.

"So," the teacher said, "first thing Monday morning, y'all

need to turn your projects into the homework basket."

She scanned the room to ensure that each student heard her message. When her eyes moved to Jermaine and Olubowale, she smiled.

"You got that, Jermaine?" the teacher asked.

"Yes, ma'am," he said, jolting to attention.

The teacher continued to scan the room.

"Now, I know that school is almost out," the teacher said. "But I want y'all to finish fifth grade strong. You're about to move into middle school, where things only get more difficult. You hear me?"

"Yes, Mrs. Morrison," the class said in unison.

"Alright, now," she said. "The bell is going to ring any minute. Pack up your things, and have a wonderful weekend."

Jermaine stood up and grabbed his backpack from under his chair. He tugged on one of Olubowale's dreadlocks to wake him up.

"Hey, man," Olubowale said. "Watch the hair."

Jermaine zipped his backpack hurriedly, while his friend packed his own with care and precision.

"Let's go, O," Jermaine said. "I wanna dip out as soon as the bell rings."

"Why you in such a hurry?" Olubowale said.

"I just wanna get my weekend started, man," Jermaine said.

The boys threw their backpacks over their shoulders and stood by the door. When the bell rang, they sprinted into the hallway and out the back door of the school. Once they reached the blacktop, they slowed their pace.

"Hey, bro," Olubowale said. "There's your girl."

Jermaine looked across the blacktop and saw Isabella standing with her friends underneath a chain-net basketball hoop. Her dark hair seemed to shine in the afternoon sunlight. Her purple backpack hung loosely off one shoulder. She spoke excitedly with her group of friends.

"Man, Isabella is *not* my girl," Jermaine said.

"Yeah, but you like her though," Olubowale said.

"So what?" Jermaine said.

"So, go talk to her," Olubowale said.

Jermaine dribbled his basketball skillfully, pretending to deflect his friend's good-natured challenge.

"She doesn't even know me," Jermaine said. "She has a different home room."

"Then why is she looking over at you right now?" Olubowale said.

Jermaine felt his nerves fire.

"Alright, bro. I'll go talk to her," Jermaine said. "Just don't pressure me about it."

"I won't," Olubowale said. "I'll just wait right her and mess around on my skateboard."

"Cool," Jermaine said. "Then we can walk home."

Jermaine picked up his basketball and strolled across the blacktop. He walked with a fabricated composure that he hoped would bring him real confidence. As he stepped within earshot of the girls, he heard Isabella speaking to them in rapid Spanish. He tried to listen in, but he didn't understand what they were saying.

Here goes nothin', Jermaine thought.

He stepped a bit closer and tried to act smooth. He pretended to walk by the group without noticing them, but at the last second, he turned toward Isabella and raised his eyebrows in acknowledgment.

"*Hola, chicas*," Jermaine said.

The girls giggled at Jermaine's bilingual attempt.

"Oh, hey Jermaine," Isabella said. "I didn't know you spoke Spanish."

Jermaine smiled. He felt his face grow warm.

"I don't, really," Jermaine said, shying away.

"Well, it was a good start," she said.

Jermaine looked nervously at the group of girls. He could feel their judgmental stares.

"What are you doing after school today?" Isabella asked.

"Uh, nothin' really," Jermaine said. "Just walkin' home with O."

"Cool," she said. "I'm walking to my grandma's house. We're making dinner for my little brother's birthday."

"That's nice of you," Jermaine said. "Well, maybe I'll see you around the way this weekend."

Jermaine waved to the group of girls, and then directly to Isabella. As he turned to walk away, he heard the group of girls giggle. He looked back at them and made brief eye contact with Isabella. He averted his eyes and felt his face flush. He tried to walk slowly and calmly, but he wanted to sprint away from the girls as fast as he could.

"How'd it go?" Olubowale said.

"Fine, I think," Jermaine said.

"I saw them looking at you and laughing as you walked

away," Olubowale said.

"Damn," Jermaine said. "They made fun of me?"

Olubowale slapped his forehead dramatically. His dreadlocks shook as he emphasized his point.

"No, dummy," Olubowale said. "That means she likes you."

"How do you know?" Jermaine asked.

"My older sister told me so," Olubowale said. "She's in the eighth grade. She knows."

He dropped his skateboard and rolled away slowly, waiting for Jermaine to catch up. They moved along the school's blacktop until they reached the opening through the chain link fence. Olubowale picked up his skateboard and walked down the short set of stairs.

The boys turned left and walked along Martin Luther King Jr. Boulevard. The old asphalt smelled hot as the afternoon sun cooked the street. Even the usually green grass was turning brown in the heat.

Jermaine loved his walk home from school. The street was always vibrant with life and people. He smelled the barbecue smoke that floated through the air from the restaurant across the street. He heard the heavy bass from a car stopped at the red light. He saw brightly colored graffiti that graced the otherwise dull brick exterior of the auto shop. He knew the Jamaican dance club would get loud tonight; it always did after dark. He heard laughter from his barbershop as they passed; its door was open to provide some relief from the heat.

One of his mom's friends passed on the sidewalk, so

Jermaine waved. Her husband gave Jermaine a supportive pat and smiled as he passed. As the boys stopped at the corner, an old green car with loud music stopped at the red light. The guy in the passenger seat nodded at Jermaine. He nodded his head in return. The light changed, and the car slowly rolled away. Jermaine and Olubowale strolled through the crosswalk. Their confidence built through the recognition and guidance they received from the older boys in the neighborhood.

"I wonder what kids on the Westside of town do when they walk home," Jermaine said.

"What do you mean?" Olubowale asked.

"You know, we just have such a cool walk home from school," Jermaine said. "We live in a fun neighborhood where we know everybody. We know who to talk to, who to stay away from, and where to go. I just wonder if those rich kids on the Westside have that same feeling when they walk home from school."

"I doubt it," Olubowale said. "You know those rich white boys don't *walk* home from school. They have drivers."

"Like a taxi?"

"No, like a butler or someone who comes to pick 'em up," Olubowale said.

Jermaine frowned.

"Like those kids on T.V., I guess," Jermaine said.

"Exactly," Olubowale said. "Like those kids on T.V."

Olubowale turned left to go to his house. Jermaine watched as he skated away. They planned to meet up later. After dinner, probably. Jermaine walked one more block and turned right. He walked across his front lawn. The dry grass crunched beneath his shoes. He jumped up the brick step and unlocked the front door to his one-level house, tossing his backpack to the side. It landed by the window; the hardwood thudded beneath the weight of the textbooks. Jermaine peeked into the kitchen.

"Mom!" He shouted. "You home?"

No one answered his call. His mom was working late tonight at the hospital; people needed nurses more frequently on Friday nights. His dad was volunteering at the community center, something he did a few nights each week as a way to give back to the neighborhood. His brother had practice after school. Jermaine would have to make dinner himself.

As he walked into the kitchen, he passed a photograph that hung from the wall; it showed Jermaine, his older brother, his mother, and his father. Though he wished they were home to greet him after school, he knew they were spreading positivity in the community.

And it meant that he had the television to himself.

Jermaine smiled and walked into the kitchen. He opened the refrigerator and grabbed the jelly. Pulling the peanut butter and bread from the cupboard, he made himself two peanut butter and jelly sandwiches. He put the sandwiches on a plate, grabbed a soda from the refrigerator, and dashed into the front room. He turned on the television and sprawled out on the couch.

"Just in time for after-school cartoons," he said.

THE WEST SIDE KID

Jonathan looked in his vintage lunch box and saw the usual contents: a peanut butter and jelly sandwich on organic bread, yogurt from free range cows, and a fair trade dark chocolate granola bar. And organic apple juice from certified trees in Spain, of course.

He sat in the back of the new black luxury car as it sped down the winding roads of the West Hills. His older sister sat in the front seat; she turned the music up loud and sang. It annoyed Jonathan; he despised the high-pitched, whiny voice of the pop artist. Or maybe it was his sister's voice that panged his nerves. He covered his ears, making a conscious effort to maintain the structural integrity of his perfectly manicured blonde hair, which he spent ten minutes combing meticulously each morning.

"Just because she's a seventh grader doesn't mean she should choose the music every day," Jonathan said.

"Now, honey," his mother said. "In two years, when you're a seventh grader and your sister goes to high school, you can pick the music."

Jonathan's sister rolled her eyes noticeably so her brother could see the action. The car pulled up to the corner of Raleigh and 26th Avenue. Jonathan unbuckled his seatbelt quickly and jumped out of the car.

"Aren't you going to say goodbye," his mother said.

"Oh, bye," he said.

He slammed the door shut. Immediately, he opened the door again.

"Hey, Mom," Jonathan said. "Can I walk home with Max after school?"

His sister rolled her eyes in the front seat. His mother looked at her, and then at Jonathan.

"Yes, honey," she said. "Just make sure you come straight home. Use the sidewalk, please. I'll be home when you get there. I'll have snacks ready."

"Thanks," Jonathan said.

He ran across the lawn and onto the playground to meet his group of friends. The first bell would not ring for another five minutes, which gave him plenty of time to talk with his friends before the rigorous academic day began.

"Hey, Jonathan," Max shouted from underneath a tree.

Jonathan walked calmly toward him and the other boys.

"Man, I can't wait until my sister goes to high school," Jonathan said. "I don't like riding to school with her."

"I know how you feel," Max said. "My big brother gets to ride in the front seat on the way to school. He has the seat warmer *and* control of the music."

"Last week, my mom told my sister that she's giving her our black car when she turns 16," Jonathan said.

Max looked around at the other boys with a perplexed expression.

"So, your sister gets a *used* car for her birthday?" Max asked.

"Well, it's new right now," Jonathan said.

"But in four years, it'll be so old," Max said. "My dad told me that I get a new car of my choice when I turn 16."

Jonathan felt his position falter. He scanned his brain for a phrase that would enhance his position within the group, but the bell rang. The boys turned and walked into the brick school building. Girls with perfectly groomed blonde hair and stylish clothes carried designer bags up the stairs; their faces were caked with makeup. Boys with trendy shoes walked around the hallways; their hair perfectly combed and gelled.

Each morning, Jonathan made an effort to look just like all the other boys at school so that he could gain the acceptance of the overall group, while asking for subtle attention by the girls. He made sure his clothes were part of the newest trends from the most popular, expensive brands. He consistently brainstormed topics of conversation that would make him appear to be at the top of the social ladder. He watched his father at dinner parties and high society events, and Jonathan emulated his strategy at a fifth-grade level.

In fact, dinner parties and country club events were the only times that Jonathan saw his father any more. He left for work early and came home late. He traveled for business meetings frequently. He missed Jonathan's last birthday. He had not been to one of his water polo games this season. Luckily, Jonathan's mother never had to work, so she was always home. She came to every game, every school event, and hosted weekly social gatherings for Jonathan's friends in their entertainment room.

Jonathan walked into the classroom with two boys who looked almost identical to him: same hairstyle, outfit, and general expression. He sat at his usual desk near the side of the room. The teacher began her daily introduction, followed by a quick-write activity. Jonathan looked out the window; his thoughts drifted.

The clock seemed to freeze; Jonathan had never experienced a longer two minutes in his life. With the end of the school day and a Friday afternoon to enjoy, he could not wait for the final bell to ring.

When it did, everyone exploded from their desks and dashed into the hallway. Jonathan ran to his locker and packed his backpack quickly. He wanted to catch Max before he walked outside; he did not want to be seen walking alone out of the school building. Luckily, Max had the same fear; he met Jonathan at his locker.

"Ready to walk?" Max asked.

"Yeah," Jonathan said. "Which way should we go?"

"I was thinking we could stop at the frozen yogurt shop on the way home," Max said. "My dad gave me fifty bucks this morning before he left for New York."

"Well, my mom told me that I had to walk straight home after school," Jonathan said. "But she doesn't have to know that we stopped."

The boys strolled down the cement steps and walked through the playground to an open grass field. The grass was pristinely groomed. Trees created shadows along the lawn; the sun sat low in the cloudless blue sky.

Jonathan saw Catherine standing near a tree on the edge of the field. His path would take him within speaking distance of her. His palms began to sweat; he rubbed them together to dry them off. Max kept up a swift pace, but Jonathan lingered as they approached the tree. He knelt down to tie his shoes, which required him to untie a perfectly secure knot. When he stood, he felt the pressure build from his stomach. He took a few more steps and decided that he had reached the optimal, casual speaking proximity.

"Hey, Catherine," Jonathan said.

"Hey," she said calmly.

"Uh, what's up?" Jonathan said.

"Just waiting for Alexis and Molly so we can walk home," she said.

"Cool, cool," he said.

He scanned his thoughts in search of another question to ask. Something to allow this conversation to continue. Max stood a few feet away, waiting for Jonathan, watching his conversational strategy.

"What are you doing after school?" Jonathan asked.

"I think the three of us were going to go see a movie," Catherine said. "Then we're having a sleepover."

"Cool, cool," Jonathan said again, immediately regretting his repetition of the phrase.

"What are you doing this weekend?" Catherine asked.

Jonathan thought about his answer. He wanted to tell her something that would make him seem cool: masculine, active, relaxed, and different from other boys.

"I have a water polo game tomorrow morning at the athletic club," he said.

"You play water polo?" Catherine said. "That's so cool. I've never seen a game before."

Jonathan smiled. He had the perfect follow-up line.

"You and your friends should come and watch tomorrow," he said.

Catherine dug the ball of her shoe into the grass. She smiled at the invitation.

"Really?" she said. "You wouldn't mind?"

"Of course not," Jonathan said. "The game's at nine at the athletic club pool."

"I'll see you there," Catherine said. "Can't wait."

She smiled as Jonathan turned and walked toward Max, who waited with an approving expression. They turned and walked across the grass. Once they reached the sidewalk, they turned west and walked to the frozen yogurt shop.

"I didn't know you liked Catherine," Max said.

Jonathan's pulse quickened.

"What? I don't," Jonathan said.

"Of course you do," Max said. "Why else would you invite her to your water polo game?"

Jonathan looked down at his feet. He tried to distract

himself by avoiding the cracks in the otherwise well-paved sidewalk.

"Don't tell anyone," Jonathan said.

"I won't," Max said. "And it's fine. I like Alexis."

Jonathan smiled. It was always safer to exchange secrets; it maintained a balance of social power.

The boys waited at the corner until the crosswalk sign indicated that they could walk. An expensive sports car waited at the red light; it received awestruck attention from the passing school kids. The boys turned left and strolled along a street lined with boutiques. Eventually, they reached the frozen yogurt shop. They filled their cups, paid, and sat at a table outside along the sidewalk.

"What do you think other kids do after school?" Max asked.

"What do you mean?" Jonathan said.

"Like, kids on the East Side," Max said. "What do kids on the East Side do when they walk home from school?"

Jonathan watched three elite high school students walk along the sidewalk on the opposite side of the street. Their clothes were expensive. Their backpacks were new. Their wallets were full.

"I don't know what East Side kids do after school," Jonathan said. "The same stuff as us, I guess."

"Have you ever *been* to the East Side?" Max said. "There's graffiti on the buildings. Their streets have giant cracks. The people over there look different than we do. It's scary."

"I guess I've never really been over there," Jonathan said.

"Well, my dad said it's a bad side of town," Max said. "He

says there are a lot of poor people over there. I bet all of those kids do bad stuff after school. I bet they're all in gangs."

Jonathan wrinkled his nose.

"Let me get this straight," Jonathan said. "You think all the fifth graders on the East Side are in gangs because they look different than us? Are you listening to yourself?"

Max lifted his chin; an aura of superiority overcame him.

Jonathan walked down the long, tree-lined driveway to his house. He looked up at the second level; its antique stonework accentuated the brick exterior. He jumped up the steps and opened the tall, dark wood door, which led to an extravagant wooden grand staircase. His mother was sitting in the kitchen at the breakfast bar. Jonathan heard her bellow from around the corner.

"I've been waiting for you, Jonathan," his mother said. "You had me worried."

"Sorry, Mom," he said. "It just took us longer to walk home than we thought."

"That's fine," she said. "Just let me know next time, please."

Jonathan looked at the floor apologetically.

"You're lucky your father's on a business trip again," she said. "Otherwise, you'd be in even bigger trouble."

She held in a smile.

"Now, go get ready for water polo practice," his mother said. "We'll leave in a half hour."

THE CALIFORNIAN

Amber took her large-frame sunglasses off and held them by her side. She did not need them in Portland's overcast mist. The old neon sign from the Southeast Theater glared at her from across Belmont Street. The sign struggled to flash in protest, its energy weakened from decades of use. Each raindrop seemed to add another layer of rust to the cracking paint on the building's exterior.

Smiling to herself, Amber walked across the middle of Belmont and approached the theater. Though she wished the theater was located on the West Side, she noticed the entrance's potential: brass handles, vintage movie lights, and an adorable ticket booth. Unfortunately for the Southeast, this potential was not part of Amber's plan.

She opened the double doors and moved with aggressive poise into the lobby. Approaching the counter, Amber asked the teenage ticket-taker to fetch the theater's owner, who promptly appeared from his back-room office.

The owner, William O'Connor, was a feeble old man who had owned the Southeast Theater since the 1960s. He loved the theater. Built in 1912, it was Portland's oldest operating movie theater, and the first in the city to host two movie screens. With the widespread megaplexes that took over the movie business many decades ago, O'Connor never made much money. When megaplexes raised ticket prices to over ten dollars, he kept his at four. He was not in the theater business for the money; he wanted to bring enjoyment to people's lives, to preserve the character of the city he loved.

But he was getting old. His heart was bad, and his lungs were worse. Smoking indoors for 55 years had given O'Connor an unfortunate respiratory system. At 75 years of age, he needed to plan for the next phase of his life: death.

"Good afternoon, Mr. O'Connor," Amber said. "It's a pleasure to finally meet you in person."

"Well, hello, ma'am," O'Connor said. "You must be that lady from California."

Amber smiled as she decided whether or not to take the comment as an insult.

"I'm Amber Marseille," she said.

She reached her hand out; O'Connor shook it with an attitude of defeat.

"I'm not sure how much you remember from our email conversation," Amber continued, "but I'm a real estate developer. My husband and I have just moved to Portland, and we'd like to purchase your theater."

The phrase jabbed O'Connor in the gut. As a former

boxer, he was used to gut punches, but this was different. He knew how to handle a typical shot to the stomach. Flex the abs, turn the body to deflect the angle, and block with the elbows. But he had seen this gut punch coming; in fact, he invited it. Still, that did not make it well-received.

"Well, I do appreciate your interest in buying the Southeast," O'Connor said. "I hadn't thought much about selling it until you reached out to me."

O'Connor had planned to leave the theater to his granddaughter when he died. His granddaughter was beginning to emerge as an influential figure in the Oregon historical community. She worked on restoring Pittock Mansion in the West Hills, and the Armory downtown. Her vision and dedication to historical preservation made O'Connor proud. But he knew that selling the theater would bring financial stability to his granddaughter when he died.

"Shall we talk about the price?" Amber asked.

O'Connor motioned for her to sit in a chair at the table in his small office. She removed a leather folder with a legal pad and began scribbling notes. Then, she ripped the paper from the pad and slid it to O'Connor.

"Here is the theater's estimated value," Amber said, gesturing to the numbers on the legal paper. "And here is what we're willing to pay you for the theater."

O'Connor's eyes widened.

"You're going to pay us almost double the value?" O'Connor asked.

"Yes we are," Amber said.

"I don't understand," O'Connor said. "Don't get me

wrong. I love the figure. But why would you pay so much more than the competition?"

Amber leaned into the table. She sensed the pride that O'Connor felt about the numbers. She wanted to play up the financial aspect of the sale to expedite the situation.

"Well, Mr. O'Connor," Amber said. "Other buyers would be purchasing your *theater*. They would probably plan to spruce it up a bit and continue to run it as a theater."

She paused for dramatic effect.

"My husband and I," Amber continued, "we're thinking outside the box. We're not interested in the theater. We want the land."

O'Connor's brow furrowed. He leaned back in his chair and crossed his arms.

"What are your plans, exactly?" O'Connor asked.

"We would tear down the theater, as you might imagine," Amber said. "It's falling apart, and no one goes to these small theaters anymore. The land that the theater stands on, however, is a prime location. We estimate that we could fit four modern-style townhouses on this lot and attract a new type of person to this neighborhood."

O'Connor shook his head in bewilderment.

"You want to tear down my theater?" O'Connor said.

"Technically, yes," Amber said. "But think of how much you could profit from this sale. We would profit from it too, of course, once the second townhome is sold. The other two sales would be pure profit for us."

O'Connor stood slowly. He fought through his arthritic knee with pride. He moved toward the table and leaned in so

Amber could hear his every word.

"Get out," he said.

"Excuse me?" Amber said.

"I'm not selling my theater to someone who just wants to tear it down," O'Connor said. "The Southeast is a piece of Portland history. It helped build its character. It still provides a place for families to spend time together in a wholesome way. I'm not selling it to you."

Amber smirked. She returned to her legal pad and scribbled out another number. She pushed it in front of O'Connor.

"What if we added another 25 percent to our purchase price?" Amber said.

Without looking at the number, O'Connor slid the legal pad back to her. He glared at Amber with ferocity. She closed her legal pad and looked down at her hands. They were shaking; she was not used to being declined. Quickly, she collected her composure, picked up her legal pad, and stood.

"Well, Mr. O'Connor," she said, "I'm confident that you'll come to your senses. And when you do, please give me a call."

Amber turned and walked briskly out of the theater. O'Connor waited until he heard the front door close before he emerged from his office. He stood behind the front counter, glaring as the Californian exited and crossed Belmont.

The door to the Southeast Theater creaked open again. A father and young daughter walked happily through the lobby and approached the counter.

"Good afternoon, sir," the father said to O'Connor.

"Hello, there," he replied, shaking the frown from his face. "What can I do for you today?"

The father looked adoringly at his daughter.

"What type of candy would you like for the movie, sweetie?" the father said.

The girl pointed at a candy box in the lower window.

"Chocolate?" O'Connor said. "That's my favorite."

He knelt down and grabbed the box of chocolate squares. He handed the box to the father, who handed it to his daughter.

"How much do we owe you?" the father asked.

"Two dollars," O'Connor said.

"That's all?" the father said. "Man, they charge an arm and a leg at the giant movie theater down the street."

He gave O'Connor two dollars, plus a one-dollar tip.

"Thanks for running an honest business," the father said.

O'Connor nodded in appreciation. The father held his daughter's hand and walked into the theater. O'Connor smiled. One of his teenage workers walked around the corner with a broom and dust pan.

"Thanks for helping them," the teenager said. "A kid spilled popcorn in the hallway, so I went to clean it up."

"I appreciate that, Bobby," O'Connor said.

The teenager returned to his post behind the counter. O'Connor walked through the lobby and into Theater Two. He found an empty chair toward the back of the room and sat down. He kicked his feet up on the chair in front of him. The animated movie began to run. O'Connor smiled as he watched the crowd.

THE SCHOOL TEACHER

With her feet kicked up on a small chair, Maryanne Hughes sat at her desk by the window in the front corner of the classroom. Papers were scattered across her wooden desktop. At first glance, the desk would appear completely disorganized; however, Ms. Hughes had a system. She knew where each and every paper was based on subject, date, and student need.

She looked out the window and watched the drizzle fall from the overcast sky. A car drove beneath her second-level window and splashed through a puddle. Ms. Hughes returned her attention to the silent fourth grade classroom. Her students were silently reading at their desks. She cherished this time; calm in the midst of chaos. Each day, she gave her students twenty minutes to free read as a way to encourage lifelong learning and literacy practice; however, the twenty minutes was coming to an end. But this wasn't all bad. The history section of the day was coming next, and she was excited to expose the kids to the story of Portland.

Ms. Hughes grew up in Southeast Portland near Benson College. Her father was a professor, and her mother ran a community garden. She spent her weekends and summers exploring the city with her mother, who taught her about the city: its highs and lows. Now, it was her turn to pass along her knowledge.

Two years ago, Ms. Hughes graduated from Portland College with her degree in education. Though she was still new to the education profession, she felt like she was starting to find a rhythm, especially since she was teaching at a school in her old neighborhood. The streets were steeped with history, color, and Portland's own culture.

Standing from her desk, Ms. Hughes rang her small bell. On cue, all of the students closed their books and placed them in their desks. Except for Matt, but that was nothing new. Two years ago, that act of defiance would have rattled Ms. Hughes, but now, she simply walked to Matt's desk and stood by him, which resulted in his immediate compliance.

"Alright, kiddos," Ms. Hughes said. "I hope you all enjoyed your free reading time today. Now it's time to shift gears and learn some history. So, please, get out your notebooks and a writing utensil."

As the students shuffled through their desks to find their materials, Ms. Hughes strolled to the front of the classroom and stood by the whiteboard. She projected a slideshow on the pull-down screen and waited for the noise to settle down.

"So, yesterday," Ms. Hughes said, "we learned that

Portland became such a popular city because it was located along a river. People used the river to fish, to irrigate their crops, and to transport materials along it using boats. Today, we'll talk about what happened in Portland from its founding until now."

Matt turned around to say something to the girl behind him. Ms. Hughes silently looked at him. Feeling her glare, Matt returned his attention to the front of the classroom.

"When Lewis and Clark left on their journey in 1804, they made it to Oregon and mapped out the land," Ms. Hughes said. "When they returned from their journey, white Americans in the Midwest heard about the fertile land. Some people began to head out to the Oregon Territory and start farming."

Ms. Hughes went on to describe the process through which Portland was founded. In 1843, Asa Lovejoy floated down the Willamette River and called the area home. Soon, Francis Pettygrove claimed some land in the area. Within two years, the settlement had grown substantially. With so many settlers coming to the new area in droves, the once forested shoreline began to look littered with stumps, which led settlers to call the city *Stumptown*. Eventually, the new inhabitants decided that the city needed an official name. Lovejoy, from Massachusetts, wanted to name the city Boston. Pettygrove, from Maine, wanted to name the city Portland. The decision came down to a coin flip, which Pettygrove won.

When Congress passed the Oregon Land Act, thousands of people made the journey along the Oregon Trail. They packed up their entire lives to claim 320 acres of land in Oregon Territory, which included modern-day Idaho, Montana, and Washington as well. So many people made the journey that wagon ruts can still be seen along the route.

After the Civil War, Portland became a major hub for timber. Due to its port and deep river, timber transportation became a major industry for the city. A railroad was created, which brought even more people to the city. But still, Portland was a rough place. Its location far away from the United States government made Portland a dense forest version of the Wild West.

As Ms. Hughes gave her students time to look at the old photos of Portland on the slideshow and continue scribing their notes, she thought about the parts of the story she was leaving out. Fourth graders would not understand the complexities of Portland's sketchy past.

She elected to omit the stories about Portland's brothels and underground opium dens. Since the city was situated on a Pacific Coast port, it had a direct line to Shanghai, which was going through its own bout with crime and corruption due to the infamous Opium Wars.

This brought Ms. Hughes's thought to the Shanghai Tunnels, an interconnected series of underground tunnels that ran beneath Portland. According to legend, loggers would come into the city each weekend to drink. Sometimes, these loggers would drink too much. Other times, they were helped to sleep by participating bartenders. These loggers would fall through trap doors into the Shanghai Tunnels, where they were captured and shuffled through the tunnels to the shores of the Willamette River. Under the cover of nightfall, kidnappers would sell them to shipping crews. The unsuspecting loggers would wake up on ships in the middle of the Pacific Ocean bound for China.

As Ms. Hughes smiled to herself, her thoughts returned to the present lesson. She told the students that by 1900, Portland had nearly 100,000 people. In fact, it hosted the World's Fair in 1905. It even had a few major newspapers. One of the newspaper owners, named Henry Pittock, became so wealthy that he built a giant mansion in the West Hills that overlooked his city.

"I've been to Pittock Mansion," Beth shouted from the front of the classroom.

"Me too!" shouted Chris.

Ms. Hughes smiled. Kids loved to share their stories and experiences, and she figured that this was the best time to do this.

"Raise your hand if you've been up to Pittock Mansion," Ms. Hughes said.

A majority of the class raised their hands.

"That's very cool," Ms. Hughes said. "Actually, next month, we're going on a field trip to learn about the history of Portland, and Pittock Mansion is one of our stops."

The class erupted in excitement. Ms. Hughes let the kids express their excitement for a few seconds before she rang her bell, which prompted the students to return to their classroom selves.

"In 1912, a wealthy businessman named Simon Benson saw that people in Portland needed fresh drinking water," Ms.

Hughes continued. "So, he donated a bunch of money to build bubbling water fountains throughout the city."

On the screen, she showed photos of Benson Bubblers throughout the city. Students whispered to each other about the ones they had seen. The Benson Bubblers still ran, cycling through with fresh water for over 100 years.

But Ms. Hughes knew the real reason behind Benson's installation of the water fountains: drunkenness. Few, if any, bars in Portland during the early 1900s served water to the hundreds of loggers that frequented the taverns. Fighting and general hooliganism began to rise, and Benson determined that the liquor had something to do with the rising crime rates. So, he installed dozens of water fountains throughout the downtown area to appease the thirst of those who would otherwise visit a tavern.

Access to free water certainly played a role in quelling the crime rate in the city, but nothing did more to *increase* it than the law meant to eliminate it: Prohibition.

When Prohibition began in Portland after the passage of the 18th amendment in 1919, people in the city still wanted a drink. The fact that alcohol was illegal probably made it more appealing to those who found new vigor after the Great War. This gave criminals, bootleggers, and building owners another avenue to make money, albeit against federal law. Secret distilleries throughout the city would covertly sell their product to building owners that ran speakeasies out of their basements or high-rise attics. Liquor barrels tended to be transported from place to place using Portland's underground tunnel system. People flocked to these speakeasies to drink, dance to live bands, and gamble. Prohibition did not stop Portland's Wild West atmosphere.

The city's criminal activity had reached a peak: gambling, prostitution, speakeasies, corruption, and opium dens. Portland's underworld became so large that it began to draw national attention. As activists for change, John and Robert Kennedy made a trip to the city to Portland to clean it up; ironically, their father had made his fortune from bootlegging as well, Ms. Hughes remembered.

"Around the time that Benson introduced the water fountains to Portland," Ms. Hughes continued, "the city started the Rose Festival. The purpose of it was to celebrate the city and the beautiful roses that grow here. The first parade was in 1907, and in 1930, they began to crown a Rose Festival Queen from a local high school."

Alicia's hand shot up from the second row.

"My cousin was the Rose Festival Queen two years ago," she said. "She went to Adams High School."

"That's very interesting, Alicia," Ms. Hughes said. "Thanks for sharing."

Alicia looked around the classroom in preparation for acknowledgement.

"Raise your hand if you've ever been to the Rose Parade," Ms. Hughes said.

Nearly every hand in the room went up. Naturally, kids began talking excitedly to their friends about the upcoming Rose Festival and their families' plans.

As the class quieted down, Ms. Hughes saw Matt raise his hand, accompanied by a look of genuine concern.

"Ms. Hughes, I've been thinking," Matt said. "You said that these two guys, Lovejoy and Pettygrove, founded the city."

"That's right," Ms. Hughes said.

"Well," Matt continued, "who lived here before them?"

THE NEW GRADUATE

D anny sat in his living room on a ragged green couch and flipped through television channels aimlessly. He saw some local news story about Portland's early history, but he wasn't in the mood or that. He wasn't sure what he was searching for, actually.

The autumn sun, although tucked behind an overcast sky, hung low above the houses. Dinner time was arriving quicker than he anticipated; his roommates would be home from work soon. He secretly envied the fact that they had jobs, however menial they were. But he told himself that he was the only authentic one. The one who wouldn't stoop. The one who would hold out to find his real passion while he lived his life. *Really* lived it.

After scanning channels one more time, Danny finally decided that he couldn't watch *Sports Talk* for a third consecutive time. He found a sweatshirt on the back of the couch, grabbed a beer from the refrigerator, and walked outside to his front porch. As he sat on the top step of the cement landing, Danny looked out at the neighborhood.

Three months earlier, Danny graduated from Oregon's largest university with a degree in business. He expected to secure a job immediately after graduation without hesitation, but for some reason, he hadn't. Neither had most of his friends. So, with little planning and money, Danny and three friends decided to rent a two-bedroom house in Portland. They wanted to live a city lifestyle after college; however, they were struggling to afford the city price tag. Downtown was not an option, so they looked on the East Side, where rental prices were cheaper. Finally, they found a run-down house in Northeast Portland that would accept their rental offer.

The house itself was old; the deteriorating paint and cracked wood siding gave it the appearance of a haunted house. The single-level home served its purpose for the boys, though. It had a living room with enough space for two couches and a television. They each had a bed, although having a roommate after college was not ideal. The front porch was big enough to sit and drink a beer. And, most importantly, it was within walking distance to some trendy bars.

And that was precisely what Danny planned to do when his roommates returned home. It was Friday night. Not that the day of the week particularly mattered to Danny. He spent his days finding freelance writing gigs online while he half-heartedly searched for a real job. He wrote a few articles per week, which gave him enough money to pay rent, pitch in for groceries, and buy plenty of beer on the weekends. Here and there, he would search for dream jobs online; most jobs required three years of experience, which he clearly did not possess.

Danny's roommate, John, had decided to make money by working as a grocery clerk while he searched for his ideal career. John worked a typical eight-hour work day a few blocks from the house, so Danny always drank a beer on the porch and waited for him to come home. Pete, the third roommate, delivered pizzas during the day. All he needed was a car and a relatively clean record. The fourth roommate, James, sold clothes at the neighborhood retail spot. He enjoyed the clientele, which consisted primarily of college girls and young professional women; however, the fact that he worked at the store they bought their clothes from produced a certain unavailable vibe.

As Danny finished his beer, he saw John turn the corner. The orange leaves on the trees began to blow in the breeze. Some fell into the street, while some fell into the perpetually wet grass that lined the sidewalk. John hopscotched over a dramatic fault in the sidewalk before looking up, catching Danny's attention.

"What up, bro," John shouted.

"Yo, yo," Danny said.

John jogged up to the dilapidated blue house, the house that he was so proud to rent. He strolled up the short cement path and sat on the bottom step.

"How was work?" Danny asked.

"Same story," John said. "Stocked some shelves. Bagged

some groceries."

He paused and looked down. Disappointment crossed his face before he quickly hid it.

"But, hey," John said, "it pays the bills until I find something I'm actually passionate about."

"I feel you, bro," Danny said.

"You hungry?" John asked,

"Yeah, real hungry," Danny said. "I was waiting for you to see what you wanted to do for dinner."

"Man, I'm thinking of a burger at the spot on Alberta," John said.

Danny nodded in agreement.

They stood from the steps and walked into the house. John changed from his work uniform to a trendier outfit.

"I'll text James and Pete and tell them to meet us there when they're done working," John said.

They strolled out the door, throwing mid-weight rain jackets over themselves to protect their clothes from the inevitable drizzle that fell from the Portland clouds. They walked through the neighborhood as the streetlights blinked on. Rain started to fall, so they threw their hoods on and walked with their heads down, but with purpose. Eventually, they reached Alberta Street, and the lights of up-and-coming dive bars illuminated the path.

An older man was leaving the burger spot as the guys approached, so Danny ducked into the restaurant as the door was closing. John was forced to remove his hands from his pockets to catch the door, braving the wet chill. They spotted a booth in the corner that looked empty, so they sat and picked up menus.

"It's happy hour for another half hour," Danny said. "Let's get a pitcher of beer and see where the night takes us."

"I'm in," John said. "Maybe we can hit up the Studio Bar after we eat. There's always fun girls there."

"James will love it," Danny said.

They ordered a pitcher of a local IPA, two burgers, and a tray of tater tots. Danny felt like a king every time he placed an order of this magnitude. Ordering a pitcher of beer and telling the server to put it on his tab gave him pride. Whether or not he was making a wise financial decision was beside the point; it made him look good on a Friday night.

James and Pete walked into the restaurant and sat in the booth. They didn't order food, just beer. Pete snacked on a few tots, but mostly just sat and talked while Danny and John ate their burgers.

When the food was gone, the server approached the table and dropped off the check. This was Danny's least favorite part of any meal. He knew that, ethically, leaving a hefty, twenty percent tip would give him social clout; however, he just demanded that the pitcher of beer be on his tab, and leaving a large tip would mean less beer at the next bar. So, he quickly scribbled the bare minimum tip of ten percent and covered the check partially with his napkin.

"Hey John, how much did you tip?" Danny asked.

"Twenty percent, like always," John said.

A wave of guilt knocked Danny in the gut.

The boys left the restaurant and walked into the cold, humid street. The rain had stopped, but the air still felt damp.

They jogged across the street to the Studio Bar. People populated a majority of the seats, but the venue wasn't too crowded yet. It was still relatively early for a Friday night. John led the group to an open space at the bar. There were only three seats, so James decided to stand.

The bartender stood behind the bar, but his back was turned. Pete shouted at the bartender to get his attention. When he didn't turn, Pete shouted again. The bartender turned and looked at the boys with reciprocal impatience. His full, black beard and paperboy hat gave him a European aura, while his full-sleeve tattoos on his forearms produced a sense of intimidation in Pete.

"What'll it be, boys?" the bartender asked.

"Four pints of that nitro stout," Danny said.

"Fine choice, lads," the bartender said.

He methodically poured the beer into the pint glasses and distributed them with efficiency.

"Would you like to start a tab?" he asked.

"Sure," John said.

He handed his card to the bartender.

James saw a group of girls approach the bar. He turned and gave an excited expression to his friends, and then returned his attention to the girls. They saw an opening at the bar near the boys and made a move to order drinks.

"What are you drinking tonight, ladies?" James asked, a smug tone in his voice.

"Not sure yet," one of the girls replied.

"Well, when you decide, let me buy your drinks," James said.

The girl smirked and discretely rolled her eyes.

"No thanks," she said.

James determined that he needed to increase his pressure.

"Independent," James said. "I like it."

The girl raised an eyebrow.

"You know," James continued, "my friends and I live just a few blocks from here. Why don't you and your friends come over and have some drinks at our place?"

The girl looked at her friends for support. One of the girls laughed audibly. Another girl ordered four drinks, which the bartender poured with a familiar efficiency.

"Listen, man," the girl said, "my friends and I just want to have a casual drink after a long week at work. We're going to let you and your boys do the same."

She paused and patted James on the shoulder.

"Enjoy your night," she said.

The girls grabbed their drinks from the bartender, turned, and walked confidently to a corner booth. James returned his attention to his friends.

"That went well," John said.

"Shut up," James said.

The boys finished their beers and ordered another round. They left their claimed spots at the bar and moved toward an open pool table. Danny, Pete, and John played a game of cutthroat, while James recovered from his rejection by leaning arrogantly against a wooden beam.

"Danny," Pete said, "I'm knocking your two ball into the side pocket."

"You better not," Danny said.

Pete hit a shot that knocked Danny's ball straight in the pocket.

"Gotcha," Pete said.

"Nice shot," John said.

The game of cutthroat carried on as each player targeted the others. Eventually, the game ended. John offered for James to take his spot in the next game, but James refused, so the three played another round.

"You know, someday, I want to own a bar," Pete said. "That's been my dream since I was in high school."

"I want to be a business owner too," Danny said. "The CEO of my own consulting business. Wear nice three-piece suits every day. Live in a big mansion in the West Hills. Drive my hot wife to tennis lessons in my BMW."

"That's the life for me," Pete said.

"Well get there," John said. "We just have to wait for our opportunity. Just be patient and play our cards right, and things will fall into place."

The bar filled with a steady stream of patrons - most were young, trendy twenty-somethings. The crowd had an eclectic style: glasses, plaid shirts, rolled-up jeans, snap-back hats, suit jackets, Blazer jerseys, and waxed mustaches. Between pool shots, Danny watched the crowd. He envied the confidence that most of these people projected. They swaggered around the bar buying pitchers and drinks for everyone. They seemed to flaunt their young success. He wished he had that same level of achievement.

As the night went on, the crowd thinned. The boys decided it was time to go home. Danny and John walked to the bar to retrieve John's card. The bartender handed the card to John along with the bill. John quickly scribbled the total amount and signed the card, placing the bill face down on the bar top.

"Thanks fellas," the bartender shouted from the other side of the bar.

"Thank you," Danny shouted.

The two boys walked through the sparse crowd to the front door to meet Pete and James.

"How much do I owe you for the drinks?" Danny asked.

"Nothing, man," John said. "Tonight's on me."

"How much did you tip?" Danny asked.

"Twenty percent, like always," John said.

"Well, can I pay you for that, at least?" Danny asked.

John put his arm around Danny.

"We're all good, buddy," John said.

As the boys walked out the front door and crossed Alberta Street, the bartender picked up the signed bill from the bar top. He looked at it to make sure it was signed, and then his eyes caught the tip line.

"No tip?" the bartender muttered to himself. "Inconsiderate punks."

The boys strolled home in a light rain. They laughed as they approached their disheveled blue house, which glowed beneath the orange streetlights. Danny sat on the couch and turned on the television. Pete sat on the other couch and immediately fell asleep.

"I'm going to bed," John said.

"See you tomorrow, bro," Danny said.

James disappeared into his room, leaving Danny essentially alone on the couch. He flipped through the channels three times, each time expecting that something different would catch his eye. Finally, he settled on *Sports Talk*. Again.

THE BARTENDER

Sean parked his small pickup on Wygant Street, just a block from the bar he worked at on Alberta. A light rain fell from the overcast sky. He threw a light rain jacket over his black button-up shirt and placed a paperboy hat snuggly on his head. He walked briskly up the sidewalk until he reached the front door of the bar.

As he entered the dark room, he removed his rain jacket and shook it off, but he decided to leave on his paperboy hat. He hung his jacket on the hook in the back room. Then, he rolled up his shirt sleeves and cuffed them snugly, which revealed his forearms that were fully covered in tattoos. Sean took pride in his tattoos; they each meant something special. His left forearm featured a large Celtic cross, a symbol of his heritage; Sean's parents immigrated to the United States when Sean was four years old. Though his own Irish accent had faded mostly, he kept his Celtic cross tattoo as a constant reminder of where he came from.

Only a few people sat in the bar's booths, but he knew that after the dinner rush ended at nearby trendy food spots, the Studio Bar would fill with thirsty patrons. He looked at his watch: 4:49. Technically, he didn't start until five, but he decided to take his post behind the bar anyway. *Ten more minutes to get tips*, he thought.

A man walked in and sat at the end of the bar by himself. Sean watched him out of the corner of his eye. He assumed that the man was at the bar by himself, and would remain alone based on his demeanor. Sullen eyes, droopy face, hunched shoulders. Everything about the man's presence suggested that he had a long week at work, and not many friends to commiserate with.

Sean finished cleaning a glass, set it down, and walked slowly to the end of the bar, where he made purposeful eye contact with the man.

"What'll it be, sir?" Sean said.

The man looked up slowly. His face displayed sadness.

"Rum on the rocks," the man said.

"You got it," Sean said.

He reached for a mid-shelf rum and poured it over ice, and then placed the drink on the bar. The man gave Sean his credit card to start a tab, implying that he would be in that seat for a while.

Sean saw the street lights flicker on outside; rain drops cascaded across light beams before splashing softly on the sidewalk. Despite the rain, Portlanders roamed Alberta Street. Trendy wanderers sought the hippest nightlife spots on the

East Side. After the dinner, Sean knew, these young bar-hoppers would find themselves in front of his bar top.

Slowly, the Studio Bar began to fill with people. It started as a trickle, as it always did. The sophisticated, after-work, happy hour crowd in their business attire showed up first. They sat at large tables in the middle of the room. *They need to be seen*, Sean thought. Gray and patterned suit jackets slung over their chairs. Top buttons on dress shirts were foregone; ties unraveled slightly to display a purposeful casualness. Women in business skirts laughed in high-pitched hilarity; this is where they blended the carelessness of their college years with the professionalism of the workforce. Halfway flirting, halfway reserved.

Sean loved to watch the business happy hour interactions unfold. As a bartender, he never participated in a traditional after work happy hour, so this was a show he could only watch from afar. The need for businessmen to impress their female counterparts on a drunken level amused him. *As if men don't try to overpower women in the business world enough as it is*, he thought.

"I'm sure you get hit on at work all the time," a male businessman said to a female coworker.

She blushed slightly and looked away.

"No, not at all," she said.

"Oh, sure you do," he continued. "Come on, you're beautiful."

Sean smirked at the irony in the conversation. He cleaned another glass to remain within earshot of the conversation before he moved to the storeroom to grab another keg. When he emerged, he noticed a female voice dominating the conversation, but somehow subtly.

He was always amazed at how some business woman fell prey to this machismo. Not all, but enough. The women who did dominate the men at happy hour did so subtly, almost so discreetly that the men could not sense it happening until they left the bar. Maybe they would not feel the dominance until work on Monday.

His favorite aspect about business happy hours came at the end: the check. Business people always wanted to impress their coworkers with picking up the check. And those who were not quick enough or bold enough to pick up the check volunteered to leave the tip. Fortunately for Sean, leaving the tip was a show of force in the business happy hour realm. Dropping a fat stack of cash as the tip showed coworkers that they were generous, and that they were a power player. Sean did not see it that way; he just saw more money in his pocket at the expense of another person's pride.

After the business happy hours subsided, the after-dinner rush came into the bar for a nightcap. Young couples on their first dinner dates. Groups of friends who wanted to act like adults and go to a trendy restaurant on a Friday night and grab a casual drink afterwards because that's what real adults did.

Sean enjoyed observing couples on first dates. He assumed that if they made it to the bar after dinner, the night was going well. The conversations were usually awkward.

"So, what do you do?" a guy would ask.

"I work in marketing," the girl would say.

Then the guy, having a job of lesser pay or lesser status,

would embellish when the question was returned.

"What about you?" the girl would ask.

"I'm in the process of starting my own thing," the guy would say ambiguously. "You know, I graduated from the business school, so that's the direction I've always wanted to go. I'm all about following my passions."

Sean had heard this conversation many times over. He laughed each time; the lack of detail, the absence of truth at the inception of a relationship. From the bar, he didn't need to hear the actual words in these conversations; he could read body language fluently. Typically, a girl forced a laugh at the guy's semi-clever jokes. The guy fished for opportunities to make himself appear more established and secure than he actually was. The guy puffed his chest to produce an aura of confidence, but Sean always looked at the feet. A nervous man tapped his feet regularly, or curled them inward as a subconscious sign of insecurity. And the girl acted in much the same subconscious manner.

While Sean received free entertainment from the first-daters during this phase of the night, he genuinely enjoyed the company of the young professional crowd: the group of college friends who now worked in the business world and wanted to do adult activities. Sean enjoyed their drink orders. They ordered cocktails that made them appear sophisticated because they saw these drinks in movies: manhattans, martinis, scotch on the rocks. He knew these young adults probably did not enjoy these drinks, but he crafted them anyway. Often, they ordered their standard college drink, like whiskey and cola, but they specified the liquor to validate their orders, substituting *whiskey* with a mid-shelf brand name. Again, this amused Sean; the soda masked the flavor of a more expensive liquor, making the upgrade useless, but he poured what they requested. He needed the money.

Besides, it forced them to leave a bigger tip, which was fine with him.

After about 9:00, the crowd tended to shift from young adults masking as professionals, to young adults reverting back to college. This crowd emerged from one bar and walked into another, and then ended up at Studio Bar. They barged in with a distinct drunken swagger. They ordered drinks in mass quantities, and shared with everyone they knew. Where the young adult professionals displayed politeness, the reverters displayed arrogance and distaste.

"Hey, man," they would shout at Sean, "gimme a pitcher."

Not a *please* or *when you have a chance*. Not even an *excuse me*.

Oftentimes, Sean played his best passive-aggressive role with these rude invaders by pretending to wash a glass and ignore them. He waited to see how low they would stoop in manners just to acquire another round of cheap drinks.

Tonight, a particularly familiar group of invading reverters barged into the bar. Sean saw them as they entered; he detested this group. Except for one. One of the boys was usually mild-mannered and respectful.

The Studio Bar was packed, so the group weaved their way through a seam in the crowd and found some space at the bar top. They ordered drinks. Then, a group of young professional women approached the bar near them. Sean could tell that these women had no interest in barbarians like these guys, but he watched in amusement as the guys tried anyway.

"What are you drinking tonight, ladies?" one of the guys asked smugly.

"Not sure yet," one of the girls replied.

"Well, when you decide, let me buy your drinks," he said.

Sean saw the girl rolled her eyes overtly.

"No thanks," she said.

The guy puffed his chest as a means to regain his footing and assert dominance over the situation.

"Independent," the guy said. "I like it."

The girl looked at him with a bewildered expression that Sean had seen hundreds of times as an observant bartender.

"You know," the guy continued, "my friends and I live just a few blocks from here. Why don't you and your friends come over and have some drinks at our place?"

The girl looked to her friends to make sure they were witnessing the hilarity.

"Can we have four vodka-sodas, please," one of the girls asked Sean.

In an effort to release the women of this embarrassing display of chauvinism, he poured the drinks efficiently and passed them to the girls across the bar top. The girl looked at Sean in acknowledgement, and he returned the expression, the non-verbal recognition of the situation.

"Listen, man," the girl said to the barbarian, "my friends and I just want to have a casual drink after a long week at work. We're going to let you and your boys do the same."

She paused and patted him on the shoulder.

"Enjoy your night," she said.

Sean turned and pretended to polish another glass. He smirked as he watched the boys through the mirror behind the bar. The look of unfamiliar defeat on the guy's face was priceless.

After a while, the bar began to wind down. Rarely did Sean have to make a last call; people in the Studio Bar just seemed to know that it was time to move on.

By this time, the drunk guys decided it was time to go home. Two guys from the group approached the bar and asked for their check. Sean gave it to them quickly in an effort to move them along. They filled out the check and slapped it on the bar top. Sean finished wiping down a section of the bar top as he watched the group of boys leave. Then, he picked up their check and moved to the register. As usual, he looked at the check to ensure that it was filled out correctly. His eyes moved to the tip line.

"No tip?" Sean muttered to himself. "Inconsiderate punks."

Sean waited until the last guest had left Studio Bar before he finished cleaning up. He locked the doors, collected his tip money, and placed the rest of the earnings in the backroom safe. He grabbed his coat and left through the side door.

Walking alone in the dark, he felt the rain begin again. He ruffled his beard to shake off the rain. When he reached his car, he paused and leaned against it. He watched the street lights as they illuminated familiar, soft rain drops.

THE BOOKWORM

Izumi stood in the corner by the window. Outside, rain fell lightly into the pockets of puddles that formed along Burnside's old sidewalks. A cyclist bypassed the rush hour traffic and jumped onto the curb, his tires splashing through puddles as he sped along the empty section of concrete. A pedestrian shouted at him as he weaved back into the street, cutting off a taxi, which honked aggressively. Izumi hardly noticed.

She was inside Quimby's Bookstore listening to a new author read a passage from a new book. Coffee warmed her hands as she leaned against the cold window at the back of the crowd. Sometimes, she wished she enjoyed going out to trendy bars in neighborhoods like Alberta, but she preferred the quiet of a bookstore and a coffee shop.

The author read the chapter with a soothing tone that almost lulled Izumi to sleep. She enjoyed listening to authors read their own work; it gave the book more authenticity. Every Thursday, Izumi went to the bookstore to listen to the week's guest author read a section of a new release, answer questions about writing, and sign autographs. Sometimes, she found interest and would purchase the book. Other times, she used the moment to think about her own creative ambitions. Today was one of those moments.

Izumi's mind wandered. As she neared age 25, it was time to start thinking seriously about how to get her work published. Or, maybe now would be a good time to start working on the documentary she had wanted to make. Either way, exploring the lifestyle of an introvert was her theme and focus. Maybe she would write a song about it? But then she would have to perform it. That certainly would not work.

Applause from the audience snapped Izumi back to the present moment. The author said she had time for a few questions; this was Izumi's favorite part of Thursday. Each time, she raised her hand to ask the same question. Every author had a different way of approaching the subject, and it gave Izumi more inspiration for one day creating something of her own to share with the world.

"What was the hardest part about writing this book?" a young boy asked from the front of the crowd.

The author crossed her arms and pondered the question, a question she already knew the answer to.

"Having the courage to get started," the author said. "I've always wanted to write a novel, and I finally had to just sit down and do it, regardless of what else was happening in my life."

She smiled and looked out at the crowd.

"And the editing," she said.

The crowd laughed politely.

The author looked around the crowd for another hand. Izumi raised hers slowly, nervously. The author stood on her toes and pointed to Izumi.

"You there, in the knit cap," the author shouted.

Izumi seemed to shrink, as she did each time she asked the question.

"With so many books out there, what makes yours worth reading?" Izumi asked.

The author wrinkled her nose. This question caught her off guard. She shifted her weight from one leg to the other, and leaned back with crossed arms.

"You know," the author said, "I think my book is real. So many authors try to over-write their stories and make them dramatic for the sake of being dramatic. My book is just about real life. I didn't have to create much; I just wrote what I knew."

Izumi nodded her head in acknowledgment. That was one of the most honest, yet boring answers she had received from an author, but it served as a solid reminder. Create what you know.

After a few more questions, the author sat down to sell and sign books. Izumi decided not to buy one, so she pushed her way through the crowd and ducked into another room. She loved to get lost in the bookstore. Quimby's had underground tunnels and random staircases that weaved through the city block to create a maze of literature. She found herself in the narrow wooden isles of the classic fiction section surrounded by familiar friends like Toni Morrison, Ernest Hemingway, and Amy Tan.

She picked up *The Joy Luck Club* by Amy Tan and flipped through some pages. She had read the book three times, but she thought about purchasing it as a creative homage to her favorite author. As the daughter of Japanese immigrants to the United States, Izumi appreciated authors like Amy Tan. It gave representation to her own voice; it enhanced her own confidence in her creativity, her story.

Realizing the futility of owning two copies of the same book, Izumi zig-zagged through the fiction section until she reached the coffee shop at the edge of the bookstore. Its corner windows provided a panoramic view of the city outside. The hustle and bustle of lights outside were quiet in the warm coffee shop. She approached the counter to order her usual: a large cappuccino.

Nick, the server, was working tonight. He worked every Thursday, which was another reason that Izumi spent her Thursdays at Quimby's. The person in front of Izumi paid and moved over to the next counter to await her drink. Nick lifted his eyes and acknowledged Izumi's presence with a friendly eyebrow raise.

"Izumi," Nick said, "what'll it be tonight?"

"Large cappuccino," she said.

She smiled nervously and looked at her shoes. Even though she had ordered from Nick every Thursday night for the last three months, she had barely said more than her drink order to him.

"I could have guessed," Nick said.

He smiled at her. She returned it, making brief eye contact before returning her gaze to her shoes. She paid and signed her receipt. Stepping sideways, she noticed that there was no one in line behind her. Nick passed the order off to another barista behind the counter and returned to his post at the register.

"So, what did you think of tonight's author?" Nick asked Izumi.

Panicked, Izumi stepped closer to the counter and scanned her brain for something coherent to say.

"She was alright," Izumi said.

"Why just alright?" Nick asked.

He's actually talking to me, Izumi thought. *I wasn't prepared for this. Stay calm.*

"Well, she was a little dull," Izumi said. "I'm sure her book was great, but her presentation was too dry for me. Not enough passion."

Nick smiled and nodded in genuine interest, inviting her to say more.

"I want to read books that writers were excited to write," Izumi continued. "I just didn't feel that from this one."

"That's fair," Nick said. "You come to a lot of these author visits, so I bet you have some serious experience with good books."

Izumi smiled, slightly embarrassed.

"I'm kind of a shy bookworm," Izumi said.

"I know," Nick said. "So am I."

Izumi shook her head in disagreement.

"Why do you think I work at a coffee shop at a bookstore?" Nick continued. "I wouldn't last a day at a major downtown coffee shop. All those business people bombarding me with orders and useless conversation. I like it here. I'm surrounded by people who actually *speak* instead of just talk."

Izumi smiled, recognizing her personality's reflection in Nick.

Another barista called Izumi's name. She moved to the other counter and picked up her cappuccino. She nodded at Nick and moved to her favorite table in the corner of the coffee shop, a table that edged between two windows so she could look out at the city without having to participate directly.

She reached into her purse and removed a book: *The Great Gatsby* by F. Scott Fitzgerald. She had read the book multiple times, but she found new purpose and relation to it with each reading.

A few pages went by and she set the book down to sip her coffee. Izumi looked at the window; the darkness outside provided a self-reflection. Focusing her eyes through her reflection on the window, she saw cars spring to life as the corner light turned green. She saw a woman walking briskly through the misty rain, her hood pulled up tight around her face. Her feet moved purposefully; each step avoided an inevitable puddle.

As Izumi returned her focus to the coffee shop, she saw Nick standing at her table. He placed a Quimby's Bookstore business card face down on the table. His phone number was written on the back of it. Izumi looked at him with confusion and hope.

"This is way out of my comfort zone," Nick said, "but I feel compelled to get to know you."

Izumi looked at him blankly, still astonished that he was talking to her outside of her regular coffee order.

"Would you want to go to dinner with me sometime?" Nick asked. "Maybe we can talk about books and being introverts."

He smiled at his own heavy-handed romanticism.

"That would be wonderful," Izumi said.

Subconsciously, she batted her eyelashes.

"Cool," Nick said. "Well, call when you want. I need to get back to the counter."

Nick scurried away from the table; his nerves increased his speed. Izumi looked at the phone number on the card and secured it in her wallet, which she placed in a strategic space in her purse.

She sipped her coffee, opened her book, and stared at the pages; her mind remained at the counter.

THE BARISTA

The misty rain glistened in the orange glow of the street lights, giving the quiet city a still aura. The glow seemed to intensify the darkness. Few people walked the sidewalks; only homeless city dwellers or devout business people. Marcos rubbed his eyes as he stepped off the train. He shoved his book in his backpack and walked groggily, tying his blue apron around his waist as he crossed Salmon Street. The sun would not rise for another three hours, but Marcos had the honor of preparing the Portland Bean coffee shop for the morning rush.

He unlocked the large glass door and turned to lock it behind him in accordance with his manager's instructions. He needed at least an hour to prepare the shop before customers began to wander in. Marcos had to prepare the pastries, grind the espresso beans, and re-clean the machinery to make sure everything functioned efficiently. If a piece of his assembly line failed or faltered, the morning rush would overtake him. At this point, he had a system that worked, if he did not mess it up.

Marcos had decided to take the early shift two months ago once school started again. He enjoyed the laid-back afternoon shifts in the summertime, when tourists would leisurely stroll into the coffee shop and order something easy, like an iced coffee. He spent most of his day drinking coffee, talking to cute girls, and reading during non-busy sections of the day.

Now that fall had arrived, he had a full class schedule up the street at Portland College, so he could not scrounge up enough free time to work during the afternoon shifts. So, he decided to take the before-school hours of 3:30 a.m. to 8:00 a.m. Even though he was exhausted, the early morning rush did bring in more tips than the lackadaisical afternoons of the summer.

After setting up his system of efficiency, he looked at the giant wall clock across from him. It hung from the only wall on the street side. Every other section where a wall might be was instead covered by wide windows that allowed Marcos to watch the city come to life. The clock read *4:45*. The massive clock served its purpose well, though Marcos always wondered whether the owner had placed it there for its function of time-telling, or for its trendy, decorative features.

Though the Portland Bean did not open for another fifteen minutes, Marcos decided to unlock the doors anyway. The time always seemed to move faster when he was interacting with customers.

As soon as Marcos returned to his post behind the

counter, he heard a bell jingle by the door, signifying the entrance of a customer. *And it has begun*, Marcos thought. A tall, white man with an expensively cut suit power-walked to the counter. He spoke on the phone with purpose, intensity, and a bit of arrogance.

"Come on, Steve," the man said into the phone. "You have to get this done today if you want to keep your job."

The man looked at Marcos and held up his index finger, indicating that he would be off the phone soon.

"Stop complaining and run the numbers," the man said into the phone.

He covered the phone and looked at Marcos.

"A large Americano," the man whispered forcefully.

Marcos nodded as the man returned to his intense phone conversation and sauntered to the other end of the counter. The espresso dripped into the cup. Marcos flicked levers and released steam. He swirled hot water in with espresso, adding just a dash of foam design to give the coffee its authentic corner coffee shop appearance. Marcos was convinced that people paid so much money for a simple coffee because of the foam designs. He walked to the other end of the counter and placed the large paper cup in front of the man, who was still shouting into his phone.

Without an acknowledgment of Marcos's existence, he grabbed the coffee and stormed out of the shop. Marcos watched the man chug his coffee and power down the sidewalk, still shouting commands into his phone.

"A *thank you* would have been nice," Marcos said.

He cleaned up a few spilled espresso grounds from the

counter and rinsed the machine's spare parts to prepare for the next customer, who entered promptly. The door's bell jingled as a young businessman strolled in. His power suit and fresh-out-of-college swagger immediately bothered Marcos. The customer's perfectly quaffed hair and entitled demeanor gave off the first impression of someone who had never had to work for anything in their life; quite the opposite of Marcos's upbringing.

As a small child, Marcos immigrated to the United States with his parents; they hid in the back of a semi-truck carrying produce across the border. His parents found work as landscapers and were paid in cash. Marcos was part of a group that the U.S. government now called "Dreamers" - he lived in the sanctuary city of Portland and had attended public school since kindergarten, becoming a high school graduate before moving on to college.

This customer, on the other hand, gave the impression that he was entitled to everything he had ever wanted. He looked like everything had been handed to him. Marcos resented him as soon as he walked in the door.

"Hey, *hombre*," the young man said. "Give me a latte."

Marcos internalized the slur.

"What size would you like," Marcos said, feigning politeness.

"Large," the young man said. "Or, what's the term you people use? *Grande?*"

"What exactly do you mean by *you people?*" Marcos asked. "If you mean baristas, we typically say *large*. If you mean college students, we also say *large*. If you mean Mexicans, *decimos grande.*"

"Woah, sorry to offend you, bro," the young man said. "It's hard to be so politically correct these days. Everyone gets offended by something."

Marcos smiled and looked the young man directly in his eyes.

"A good rule of thumb," Marcos said, "treat people with respect."

The young man looked at Marcos as if he had never been talked to that way before. He paid quickly and scampered to the other end of the counter. Marcos crafted a latte and placed it on the counter.

"*Su cafe, jefe,*" Marcos said.

"Uh, thanks," the young man said.

Marcos smiled as the young man fumbled his way out of the coffee shop. The orange street lights outside flickered, a signal that they would soon turn off as the sun began to rise. The bell jingled. Marcos's head snapped toward the door as a trained reflex. In walked a man that looked exceptionally disheveled. His black hair was matted into dreadlocks, not as a fashion statement, but a result of limited access to a shower and shampoo. His face was heavily bearded, and his black skin was covered in city grime. His coat hung to his knees, exposing his torn jeans and worn boots.

Homeless people frequented the coffee shop. Marcos knew what this man was after: money. He knew the man would come in, tell some fabricated sob story, ask for money, and use it to buy alcohol at the liquor store around the corner. As the man approached the counter, Marcos was ready with his usual strategy for dispelling homeless people.

"Good morning, sir," the man said to Marcos.

"Good morning," Marcos said. "What can I do for you?"

The man looked at the menu. Marcos knew the man was not really looking at his ordering options.

"I wanted some breakfast, but I don't have enough money," the man said.

"Not a lot we can do about that, unfortunately," Marcos said.

The man looked at Marcos with human suffering.

"Any chance you could spare a dollar?" the man asked.

"Sorry, sir," Marcos said. "I can't give you anything from the cash drawer. Company policy."

The man nodded and seemed to accept this answer. He rubbed his stomach, indicating real hunger. Marcos noticed and tried an old trick to see if the man was truly hungry, or simply wanted money to feed his vices.

"I'd be more than happy to give you a coffee and a bagel though," Marcos said.

Marcos eyed the man's reaction, assuming he would turn down the offer. The man looked at Marcos with genuine compassion.

"You would do that for me?" The man asked. "Why? You don't even know me."

"If you're hungry, I'll feed you," Marcos said.

The man folded his hands in gratitude.

"Sir, that would be lovely," the man said. "I haven't eaten in two days."

Marcos smiled in surprise; he loved that his assumption

was wrong.

"I'll have that order right up for you, sir," Marcos said.

He thought about simply pouring the man some drip coffee, which would have been cheaper, but he looked at the man's genuine gratitude and decided to create a real espresso concoction. Marcos crafted a foam heart to top off the drink. He toasted the bagel, and then placed the coffee and food on the counter. The man approached the counter cautiously, looking at Marcos for reassurance.

"It's all yours, sir," Marcos said. "On the house."

The man began to cry.

"Thank you so much," the man said through soft sobs.

"It's my pleasure," Marcos said.

The man walked slowly away from the counter and out onto the sidewalk. The sun was beginning to light up the city streets. Marcos watched through the windows as the man strolled away with a smile on his face; a single tear glistened in the sunrise.

THE OLD WOMAN

Ruby sat in the corner of Sal's as she waited for her sister, Marion, to arrive. They agreed to meet at three, but Marion was always late, so Ruby ordered a drink to pass the time. The well-dressed server brought a gin martini to the table and placed it elegantly in front of Ruby.

"Thank you, young man," Ruby said.

"Can I get you anything else, ma'am?" the server asked.

"Oh, heavens, no," Ruby said. "I'm just waiting on my sister."

The server nodded and walked efficiently back to the bar. Ruby watched him as he left. The servers here still wore the same outfits they had worn for the last fifty years, if not more. Red waistcoats, white shirts, and armbands. In fact, the decor probably hadn't changed much over the last ten decades or so. The dark wood paneling accented by golden fixtures and red velvet cushions provided an ambiance of a bygone golden era.

Sal's opened in 1895, making it the oldest bar in Portland; Ruby and Marion hadn't been coming here *that* long, of course, but it sometimes felt like it to Ruby. She looked around the bar and wondered what misgiving stories had occurred in these very walls throughout the bar's long history.

As Ruby took the last sip of her drink, she saw Marion walk through the front door. She shook off her raincoat as she placed it on the hook. Ruby leaned back in her chair and waved half-enthusiastically at her younger sister. Marion sat across from her and breathed a heavy sigh of apology for her typical tardiness.

"I'm glad you finally made it," Ruby said. "I was getting worried about you."

"Oh, stop it, sister," Marion said. "You know I'm always fashionably late."

She smirked at Ruby, who feigned a scoff.

"Besides," Marion continued, "I couldn't find a place to park. There are so many people downtown these days. Then I spoke with the nicest young man who was just getting off of his shift at a coffee shop a few blocks down. Boy, was he cute. If I was a few years younger…"

"Sister, you would," Ruby said. "Where'd you end up parking?"

"Oh, six blocks away or so," Marion said. "All these people taking up my usual spots."

They discussed their distaste for all of the people moving up to Portland from California. Marion rattled off statistics about how many families were moving to Portland from other states, and how many jobs they were stealing, and how many cars were added to the freeways each week. Whether these statistics were accurate or not was another matter entirely.

The server arrived. Marion ordered her usual: a turkey sandwich and a gin gimlet. Ruby couldn't stand gin gimlets, but she did order another gin martini with a turkey sandwich.

"We're products of a bygone era," Ruby said. "Look around. All these young, trendy folks coming to Sal's for a vintage experience. Heck, we just came here because it was the bee's knees."

"Sal's really was the place to be seen when we were in our heyday, wasn't it?" Marion said.

"Say, you remember when we met those two brothers here for a drink in '63?" Ruby asked.

"I sure do," Marion said. "We sat in that corner booth."

Marion smiled, pointing to the corner booth where four young friends sat and drank craft beers.

"Boy, were those brothers handsome," Ruby said. "What were their names? Michael and Seamus?"

"Yes, ma'am," Marion said. "The Fitzpatrick brothers. Why on Earth did we stop seeing them?"

Ruby threw her arms up in retrospective protest.

"Daddy wouldn't let us because they were *goddamn Catholics*," Ruby said.

Marion rolled her eyes and reached for a bread roll. The server returned with their drinks, and soon after, he returned with their turkey sandwiches. Marion added a splash of mustard to hers. Ruby, however, liked her turkey sandwich just the way the chef made it.

Marion took a bite of her turkey sandwich, and then immediately began to laugh as another memory surfaced. She chewed quickly so she could speak.

"Remember when we drove to North Portland and met those two fellas who worked at the shipyards?" Marion asked.

"How could I forget?" Ruby said. "Those two gentlemen showed us a real good time. I haven't danced like that ever in my life."

"And here I thought we knew the city, until they showed us the East Side of the river," Marion said.

"Why did we stop seeing them?" Ruby asked.

"Don't you remember?" Marion said. "Daddy didn't like them because they were *poor East Side bastards.*"

Ruby rolled her eyes and took a drink from her martini glass. It was a different time then, the sisters recalled. A time when differences, no matter how trivial, were seen as obvious division. A time when maintaining one's social image was a family's main priority next to food, water, and shelter.

"Oh, how times have changed," Marion said.

Marion's comment lingered in Ruby's thoughts. Ruby looked across the room to a booth where a black girl and a white boy held hands as they waited for their lunch to arrive. She heard a group of friends speaking Spanish with one another in casual conversation. Through the window, she saw a Muslim woman walk down the sidewalk with a headscarf. During the era of her vibrant youth, these sights and sounds did not exist. At least in Ruby's world.

"Times do change, sister," Ruby said. "Just look at these

wrinkles on my hands. I sure didn't have these when we were living in that apartment building around the corner fifty years ago."

"I find it harder and harder to change with the times," Marion said. "I look around and see people that seem younger and younger. Their ideas feel so progressive. Meanwhile, I'm still stuck trying to play catch-up."

Ruby nodded and sighed in agreement.

The server brought the bill and placed it on the table in a distinguished leather-bound billfold. Marion declared that it was her turn to buy lunch, but Ruby insisted it was her turn. The server mentioned that they could easily split the bill through their system. Seeing this opportunity to compromise, the sisters agreed to split the bill.

They stood and walked toward the door. Marion put on her raincoat, while Ruby placed a knit cap on her head. As they prepared to leave, a young, dapper man approached the door from the outside. He smiled, opened the door, and nodded to the sisters as they thanked him. They watched him enter Sal's, making sure the door closed behind them, before they giggled.

THE WAITER

Turner stood in the industrial kitchen at Sal's, waiting impatiently for the cook to finish spreading potato chips over the empty side of the sandwich plate. His customers at Table Seven had waited long enough for their late lunches. They hadn't complained; it wasn't Portlanders' style to complain about slow servers. But they were on their second round of beers without food, and he knew that they were growing anxious. Plus, he wanted a good tip to supplement his barely-above-minimum-wage paycheck.

As he watched his customers look around the restaurant hungrily, the cook rang the bell, which indicated that the meals were ready. Turner grabbed the sandwich plates and hustled to their table.

"I'm so sorry about the wait, y'all," Turner said to the young man and woman. "We're short one cook today, so we've been moving a little slower than we're used to."

"It's alright, bro," the young man said.

The customer's thick-rimmed glasses and squat beanie defined Portland style, a sharp contrast to Turner's usual khaki shorts and boat shoes.

"How'd y'all like those beers?" Turner asked.

"They were good," the young man said.

Turner smiled.

"You know, that stout you had was rated one of the best beers in the city," Turner said. "It's surprisingly complex. Chocolate aroma and coffee notes on the front end with a hint of cherry on the back. It's from a cool new brewery just down the street. But I'm sure y'all Portlanders already knew that."

The man nodded his head a bit too eagerly in an attempt to indicate his awareness of brewery understanding. His face, however, showed Turner that his knowledge was quite limited.

"You said *y'all*," the young woman said. "Where are you from?"

Turner felt himself blush. He knew that his southern drawl revealed his un-local status every time he spoke.

"I'm from Tennessee," Turner said. "I just moved here about a month ago."

The young woman looked him up and down and smiled approvingly. The young man leaned back in his chair and rubbed his patchy beard, feeling slightly out-manned.

"What brought you all the way out to Portland?" the young woman asked.

"Hopes and dreams, darlin'," Turner said.

She smiled, enchanted by his accent. Turner reciprocated.

"Naw, I just graduated from a college in the South," Turner continued. "I drove to Portland to find work in the craft brew industry."

Turner rolled his eyes to deflect the fact that he had yet to make progress in finding a job within his chosen field.

"Well, this is the place to do it," the young man said.

Turner nodded, catching the young woman smiling at him flirtatiously, out of view of her boyfriend. Turner returned the smile and walked back to the kitchen to retrieve the next order: a gin martini. He grabbed the drink and walked to a table where an elderly woman sat alone waiting for her sister to arrive.

When the elderly woman's sister finally showed up and sat at the table, Turner took their food orders. After placing them with the kitchen, he walked to the table next to them and cleaned the crumbs from the empty table so he could flip it for the next customer. Though he usually worked quickly, he was intrigued by the conversation taking place at the elderly women's table, so he slowed his pace and eavesdropped.

They began discussing their distaste for all of the people moving to Portland from other parts of the country. They complained that these people were clogging up the freeways, taking all the parking spots downtown, and generally making life in Portland miserable for all of the "true Portlanders".

Turner began to fume; this was a conversation topic that he had heard multiple times since moving here. It contradicted everything he thought of the city before moving here. He assumed that everyone in Portland was so hospitable and welcoming; instead, he found that most Portlanders thought that outsiders were disturbing their peaceful city. He did not feel welcome; he felt unwanted.

His decision to move from Tennessee to Portland was not an easy one. He was leaving everything he knew behind him. He was born and raised in Tennessee: his family, his friends, his tradition, and in many ways, his identity. He did not move to Portland to be an inconvenience; he moved here to be a part of something exciting. The craft brew industry was a passion of his, and he wanted to live in its epicenter.

As he continued to clean the table, his building internal rage morphed into melancholy. He trudged his way back to the kitchen to retrieve the elderly women's order. His eyes felt heavy. His posture sagged. Two turkey sandwich plates sat in the window ready to serve. Turner wanted to spit on the bread, or add hot sauce, or do something that would cause them to regret their dislike for him. He eyed their drinks that sat next to the plates: a gin gimlet and another gin martini. Maybe he could spit in their drinks? They'd never know.

But he would.

He picked up the gin martini; saliva built up in his mouth. He pulled the drink closer to his face, and paused.

Fighting hatred with revenge was not the way to approach this situation. He needed to win the people of Portland over, not give them reasons to dislike outsiders. He loaded the plates and drinks on his serving tray, plastered on a polite smile, and bounded his way to the women's table.

"Your sandwiches, ladies," Turner said. "And your cocktails."

"Thank you, young man," one elderly woman said.

"Will that be all for you lovely ladies?" Turner said, amplifying his southern accent.

"No, thank you," the woman said.

"Well, it sure has been a pleasure for this Tennessee gentleman to serve y'all," Turner said. "If there's anything at all I can do for you, just let me know."

The sisters looked at one another with approving expressions. As he walked away, he heard them giggle, though he wasn't quite sure why. Eventually, he brought them the bill, which they split. He returned their final checks in the Sal's signature leather billfold, thanked them again, and wished them a pleasant afternoon. After he saw them fully exit the restaurant, he returned to their table to grab the checks. As he opened it, he saw two fifty-dollar bills left for him as a tip.

THE HISTORIAN

Dr. Taylor squinted his eyes in the dark room in the depths of the building. He scoured the drawers of dense file cabinets that seemed to go on forever. After sifting through the last folder in the cabinet, he moved on to the next one. He knew he was close to finding the document he needed.

In the digital era, I'm still back here searching for a simple paper document, Dr. Taylor thought.

He thumbed through the middle of the file cabinet until he found it: a primary source of a police record from 1925. He closed the file cabinet, locked it with a key from the ring attached to his belt loop, and returned to his office. He set the old police record on his desk and walked into the main hall of the Oregon Historical Society before making his way into the coffee shop, where he ordered a mocha. He needed the caffeine to continue working at this pace. He woke up at

4:00 a.m. so that he could exercise and be at his desk by 5:30 to continue his breakthrough progress on his research.

With the prospect of work fueling his nerves, he decided to pause and enjoy the morning for just a moment. He sat at a corner table to wait for his coffee order and watched people bustle through the coffee shop attached to the museum. School children on field trips, old folks meandering through the city on vacation, and college students on research missions.

He saw a waiter that looked familiar from one of his favorite bars in the city. He enjoyed that bar for its historical significance. And they served a fine manhattan.

Dr. Taylor looked at some of the video displays on the wall of the main hall; his own research scanned across the screen. He smiled, proud of his accomplishments.

Before the age of 35, Dr. Taylor had earned his doctoral degree in history, an achievement he never thought he could reach until he did it.

He recalled his doctoral dissertation, a piece that shed light on a segment of history that many Oregonians would have liked to forget. He researched the causes and effects of the state's constitutional policy that barred African-Americans from living in Oregon until 1922, making it the only "whites-only" state under United States sovereignty. His groundbreaking research brought in historians, documentary filmmakers, writers, and journalists from across the country to use Dr. Taylor's research in their respective projects, enhancing his well-deserved reputation as a rising historian.

His accolades and awards brought him nationwide

fellowships and job offers, but he chose to remain in his home state of Oregon, where he became the first African-American Senior Historian on the West Coast. His mother couldn't have been prouder.

"I have a mocha for Dr. Taylor," the barista shouted through the coffee shop.

Dr. Taylor stood from his table and grabbed his coffee, thanking the barista, who returned the comment with a genuine smile.

"You're Dr. Taylor," the barista said. "The Senior Historian here, right?"

"I am," Dr. Taylor said humbly.

"It's an honor to meet you, sir," she said. "I just finished my history degree down in California. I'm just working here until I can find a job in the history field."

Dr. Taylor smiled, recalling his own difficulty finding a job in the industry.

"Just keep working at it," Dr. Taylor said. "It's a tough industry to break into, but you can do it. Just be persistent."

"Thank you, sir," she said. "Enjoy your coffee."

Dr. Taylor nodded and returned to his table. A mother and her son walked into the exhibit area. The mother held her son's hand as she led him to the introductory video screen. Dr. Taylor watched as they explored the interactive history lesson on the screen, a lesson that was fueled by more of Dr. Taylor's research. The mother read the passages out loud so her son could follow along. Their excited conversation gave Dr. Taylor another reason to smile.

A young man walked briskly by the family and approached

the coffee shop. He stood next to Dr. Taylor's table, adjusted his glasses, and cleared his throat to get the Senior Historian's attention.

"What's up, Bobby?" Dr. Taylor asked.

"Dr. Taylor, I know I'm supposed to be working on the Pittock Mansion project," Bobby said, "but I'm wondering if I can have some free time to work on a little passion project of my own."

Dr. Taylor sipped his coffee and looked approvingly at Bobby.

"Tell me about the project, Bobby."

"Well, I wanted to look at the history of migration into the city of Portland," Bobby said. "I want to focus on the factors that brought people here. Portland is booming. People are still moving here in droves. Modern Portlanders are acting like this is some new phenomenon. But I don't think it is. It's been happening since the city was founded."

Dr. Taylor elongated his face and nodded, ruminating over the possible directions this project could go.

"I was thinking I could look at different groups: ethnic, socioeconomic, regional," Bobby continued. "I want to look at who came here and why. Maybe the descendants of those groups will find some connection with why they're here."

Taking another sip of his coffee, Dr. Taylor smiled slowly; his vision for this project began to grow.

"Bobby," Dr. Taylor said, "I love that idea. As long as you continue to make progress on the Pittock Mansion project, you have my approval to move forward with your migration project as well."

Bobby's eyebrows lifted above the rims of his glasses. He stood on his toes and clenched his fists before regaining his composure.

"Thank you, Dr. Taylor," Bobby said. "I really appreciate you."

As Bobby sped through the exhibit hall, Dr. Taylor reclined into his chair and recalled his own passion projects over the years. His first one had to do with the shipyards in North Portland. His own father worked in the shipyards for decades, so he always had an interest. Then, he thought about his current passion project. One that might garner some pushback from Portland's politicians. But he didn't mind. He was used to facing adversity.

Standing from his table and buttoning his suit jacket, Dr. Taylor strolled through the coffee shop, across the main hall, and back into his office. He sat down at his desk and began to analyze the police record he had uncovered.

Dr. Taylor had already assembled some key pieces to the puzzle, but he needed one more solid piece of evidence to support his findings. He had already discovered that Portland's Chief of Police during Prohibition ran a speakeasy out of his basement at his house on Southeast 42nd Street off of Hawthorne. Dr. Taylor uncovered evidence that he acquired his illegal alcohol by arresting bootleggers and using the confiscated alcohol to run his own speakeasy. He also knew that one of the biggest crime bosses in the city during that era, John Cleary, happened to be the brother-in-law of the Chief of Police. Yet, there was something missing from the story. Something just wasn't adding up.

He read and re-read the police report from 1925 that detailed every arrest made relating to Prohibition; Dr. Taylor knew he would find it because each state was required to report their statistics to the Federal Government regarding Prohibition. As he re-read the middle section of the source, he paused, and then snapped his fingers with assurance.

"I knew it!" Dr. Taylor shouted.

An intern scampered into Dr. Taylor's office with excitement.

"What did you find?" the intern asked.

"Cleary was never arrested for anything relating to Prohibition," Dr. Taylor said. "Cleary was arrested seven times in 1925, but none of his arrests were recorded as having to do with bootlegging or producing alcohol."

The intern looked at Dr. Taylor with a puzzled expression.

"The Chief of Police knew that any crimes involving bootlegging would be reported to the Federal Government, and Cleary would have to serve serious time in prison," Dr. Taylor said. "That would really mess up his speakeasy operation."

The intern nodded vigorously, but still did not quite grasp the significance of this finding.

"On the record, Cleary was arrested for petty misdemeanors, like *loitering* and *fighting*," Dr. Taylor continued. "This proves my theory: the Chief of Police was a business partner with Cleary."

The intern looked at Dr. Taylor quizzically.

"Don't you see?" Dr. Taylor said. "The Police Chief would arrest Cleary, take his alcohol, sell it at his basement speakeasy, but he would only make Cleary spend a few hours in jail or give him a small fine. This was how Cleary distributed his alcohol across the city: through crooked cops. To the Federal Government, it still looked like Portland Police were being tough on crime, but in reality, the Portland Police were *the* distributors for the biggest crime boss in the city!"

The intern began to nod his head vigorously as the historical implications became clear. Dr. Taylor handed him the police record and he scampered off to make a digital copy.

Dr. Taylor began to type fervently; now that he had his final piece of evidence, he knew he could present this to the Oregon Historical Society review board by tomorrow. Then, he could publish his findings in the magazine. *No*, Dr. Taylor thought, *this will be the basis for my first major non-fiction book. I can change the city's landscape with this revelation.*

Regardless of how he decided to disseminate this incredible, hidden piece of Oregon history, Dr. Taylor knew that he was one step closer to uncovering the untold story of Oregon, the story that remained purposefully hidden by those who wanted to remain anonymous, those who were ashamed of their past.

THE POLICE OFFICER

Robert pulled his police car along the curb on North Ainsworth Street. He rolled the car slowly to a stop. The street lights flickered on one by one down the block. He sat in his car for a minute to assess the environment before he exited his vehicle.

He opened his door and stepped onto the street, moving quickly yet calmly to the sidewalk, just out of range of the nearest orange glow from the street light above him. He checked the stability of his radio clip, and then moved his hand to his belt to check that his gun was securely locked in place.

Just another routine patrol route on another routine night shift. He needed to get out of the precinct anyway. The Captain had just enhanced tension at the precinct when he mentioned that a major historical scandal was coming that would make the department look bad. *What's new*, he thought.

Robert had been a cop for more than 15 years. He enjoyed the day shifts; crime seldom happened during the day. Most of his day shifts included moving homeless people from their temporary residences in building doorways, or making appearances at elementary schools to give the department a good name.

But the night shift was different, especially in this part of town. The street lights seemed dimmer. The sidewalks were rougher. And the people looked at him with a bit more of an edge than he was used to downtown.

Robert signed up for this posting in North Portland when he was a younger cop, when he still had that attitude of being a superhero. He wanted to work in North Portland, to help fix the broken community he had heard so much about as a suburban kid. He had heard that North Portland was full of gang violence, and he wanted to use his power as a cop to make a positive impact in an underserved community by exterminating the gangs, the drug dealers, the thugs.

But Robert was a long way removed from that young, vibrant cop of yesterday. He was grizzled, slightly jaded. He had seen how the law really operates, the myth of a fair trial, and the corruption that infiltrated even the most honest people on the force.

He also saw how his very presence in this community exacerbated the problem of tension. As a white cop in a black neighborhood, he knew that he was automatically perceived as the enemy, and for good reason. Robert's coworkers, his peers, so often jumped to conclusions about the people in this community simply because of rumors, of decades-old prejudices that permeated white society.

And, as much as Robert wanted to be the superhero, he knew that he was just as susceptible to this type of thinking. He knew that he might be part of the problem. And he frequently pushed this thought out of his mind, telling himself that he was there to serve, to help, to rebuild.

As he walked alone down Ainsworth, he neared Peninsula Park. The outskirts of the park were illuminated in an orange glow from the street lights, but the park's interior was dark, foreboding.

He saw a figure emerge from the shadows of a park walkway. Robert stopped and shifted his mindset to protection mode, analyzing all aspects of the figure. The figure was hooded with a dark sweatshirt; face shadowed and obscured. Backpack. Adult male. Hands in pockets. Eyes low.

Robert instinctively placed his hand on his gun. He disengaged the safety and grasped the gun with tension, ready to draw and shoot at any sign of a threat from the slowly approaching figure.

Adrenaline coursed through his hands. He positioned his body at a 45-degree angle to the figure and stood solidly on the balls of his feet, steadying his balance, ready to draw.

The figure froze. He removed his hands from his pockets, showing empty palms. He removed his hood to reveal a teenage face. He removed his headphones and looked up.

The kid's eyes met Robert's. Sheer terror exuded from his face as he saw Robert's hand on his gun. The kid put his hands straight up in the air and instinctively dropped to his knees. Panic babbled from his lips. A tear fell from his left eye.

Robert's gut dropped. He reclipped the safety latch on his holster and removed his hand from his gun. Robert showed his own empty palms, a small sign of apology. With an entirely new demeanor, Robert approached the kid.

"Hey, buddy," Robert said. "I'm sorry to scare you like that. I just got nervous myself, you know?"

The kid wiped tears from his face, sniffling quietly as he tried to regain his sense of humanity.

"Why'd you have your hand on your gun, man?" the kid said. "What did I do?"

"Nothing," Robert said. "You didn't do anything."

He paused as he tried to let silence rescue the moment. Too awkward. Too guilty.

"What are you doing in this park after dark," Robert asked.

"Just walkin' home, man," the kid said. "It's not like we got a curfew."

"You're right," Robert said. "Where are you coming from?"

The kid looked directly into Robert's eyes with purpose and determination.

"I'm coming from tutoring," the kid said, nodding toward his backpack. "I tutor middle school kids at the community center every Wednesday after school."

Guilt punched Robert in the stomach. How could he have assumed this kid was causing trouble? Was he really becoming a product of his own aggressive police environment? As he looked at the kid standing nervously on the sidewalk, he knew the answer already.

"Look, kid," Robert said. "I'm really sorry for scaring you like that. I know I'm a cop, and I know that a lot of us haven't been good to this neighborhood. And I'm sorry for that. I hate to be just another white cop. That's not what I want for me, for my profession, and especially for you."

The kid raised an eyebrow at the cop.

"But that's exactly what you doin', man," the kid said. "You can talk about justice all you want, but the action that we see from people like you in this neighborhood tells us somethin' different."

Robert's heart dropped. He knew the kid was right.

"I know," Robert said. "I promise I'll be better. I promise *we'll* be better."

He nodded at the kid, who returned the nod, albeit skeptically. The kid cinched up his backpack and continued his walk down the block to his house. His pace quickened. Robert watched as the kid moved into the orange glow of the street lights before he faded again into darkness.

THE MAYOR

Garrett sat forward in the leather chair in his office. He shoved his face into his hands and leaned against the wooden desk. The hum of the computer monitor seemed to echo through the empty room; the wall clock ticked with each passing second, reverberating off of the wooden floorboards.

The office secretary stomped down the hall purposefully. Her heels clicked louder as she approached the office. With a stack of papers in her hands, she lightly knocked on the ajar office door before entering.

"Mr. Mayor," she said, "I have a call in for you from the labor union."

Garrett left his face in his palms. He closed his eyes in frustration, but his hands covered his emotions. Slowly removing his face, he looked at his secretary with a pleasant expression.

"Thank you, Leslie," he said. "Tell them I'll return their

call in a half hour."

"You got it, Mr. Mayor," she said.

She paused before giving him the next schedule update.

"And a visit from the Fair Treatment Organization," she said. "They want to talk about an incident that happened yesterday involving an unarmed teenager and a city cop."

The Mayor rolled his eyes.

"Another one?" he said. "I don't have time to deal with something that insignificant."

The secretary raised her eyebrows in opposition, but quickly recoiled them, seeing the Mayor's rising agitation. Stomping away with her trademark walk, the secretary left the door ajar as she moved down the hall. The Mayor rose from his chair and looked out the window onto the streets of downtown.

Hundreds of protesters covered the streets along the Park Blocks. Through his window, the Mayor heard unified chants and sporadic shouts. He saw handmade signs with clever quips. And all the protestors had one goal: force the Mayor to increase minimum wage.

Garrett knew this, of course. Protest leaders had planned this event weeks ago, and the Mayor's office was informed of the protest demands well in advance. The Mayor and his team had crafted a plan that included a speech and a show of support for the protestors, who represented the working class of Portland.

The Mayor also knew that he had a group of major campaign donors who did not come from working class backgrounds. In fact, these major donors came from families and businesses that benefited heavily from a low minimum wage. Many of his voting supporters came from families that did not work in minimum wage jobs.

Garrett was one of those Portlanders himself. As a middle-aged white man, Garrett had a pathway to success from an early age. His parents were both lawyers who lived in the West Hills in a luxury home and could afford private school in the area. Whether or not the education at that school was worth the money did not concern Garrett's parents; it was the connections to other wealthy families that subconsciously motivated their decision. When Garrett turned 16, he received a new car from his parents. When he graduated from high school, he attended a small-yet-prestigious private college on the East Coast; his parents paid for the entirety of his tuition.

When Garrett returned home from college, his parents purchased a small condo on the East Side of downtown for Garrett to live in. Through his parents' connections, Garrett was given a job as a paralegal in a law office in one of Portland's tallest buildings. With no debt and no bills to pay, Garrett began law school, which he finished quickly. After spending a decade as a prosecuting attorney for a high-profile law firm, Garrett decided to take the next step in his family's legacy: he ran for mayor. The campaign proceeded smoothly; Garrett's family had curated a wealthy, influential circle of friends, which Garrett's campaign was able to exploit. With more campaign finances than any of his opponents, Garrett won the campaign by a landslide.

Winning the title of Mayor was much easier for Garrett

than the daily mayoral proceedings, though. His decision-making skills were minimal, and his ability to empathize with anyone outside of his own social class was difficult. But, Garrett recognized, his ability to understand business interests was a learned skill he had acquired from his time as a white-collar prosecutor.

The Mayor looked outside at the protestors and smiled at their innocence. They assumed that a higher minimum wage would make Portland more affordable for their working-class families. But how little they understood the complex economic systems of a city. Garrett knew what was in their best interest. He knew that if the minimum wage increased, the cost of milk and bread would increase, too. The cost of gas, taxes, and homes would increase. So, really, an increase in minimum wage would be worse for these poor people outside.

But he could not actually *say* that to them. He needed these unfortunate working-class families to feel heard. He needed these people to feel the Mayor's support. He needed these people to reelect him next year.

So, the Mayor and his team devised a speech that would give the appearance of support, a speech that would give the appearance that this protest actually meant something. If the Mayor spoke about his real plans and motivations, the protests would only grow stronger, and they might even become national news, which Garrett wanted to avoid.

Of course, the Mayor had no intention of supporting a minimum wage increase. But his speech was crafted in such a way that it gave the appearance that he did without specifically saying it. His speechwriter selected specific words and phrases that gave the illusion of support for the working class without committing to anything concrete in terms of public policy.

A heavy knock on the office door turned Garrett's attention away from the mob of protestors. His speechwriter and public relations specialist entered the room.

"I've finalized the revisions to your speech, Mr. Mayor," the speechwriter said.

"Thank you, Simon," Garrett said.

The public relations specialist took an assertive step forward.

"I know the intentions of the protestors is to secure an increase in minimum wage," the man said. "But what they really want is to feel respected. Remember, when you give this speech, you're not only talking to the protestors, but to thousands of people at home who empathize with the protestors. Come across as warm, caring, and like you are a member of the working class yourself."

The man looked at the Mayor's outfit.

"Lose the tie," he said. "Unbutton the collar, and roll your sleeves up. And we've got to ruffle your hair a little bit. Let's make it look like you're one of them."

"Thanks, Mark," the Mayor said.

The Mayor's secretary returned to the office.

"Mr. Mayor, I'm just reminding you to return the labor union's phone call," she said.

"Thanks, Leslie," the Mayor said. "Get them on the phone right now. I'll talk to them just before my speech."

"That's a great idea, Mr. Mayor," the public relations specialist said. "Sound empathetic and accommodating to their requests, but don't commit to anything specific. And be sure to remind them that you're speaking to the protestors soon to assure the working class that the City of Portland is on their side."

"Even though we all know that throwing money at poor folks won't do anything to build more roads and skyscrapers around here," the speechwriter said slyly.

The Mayor picked up his phone and smirked at his core public relations team. When the labor union representative picked up, the Mayor's face shifted to an empathetic smile.

"Hey, there, Bill," the Mayor said. "I'm sorry I missed your call earlier. I was in a meeting trying to nail down the needs of our protestors outside."

The Mayor nodded and rolled his eyes as the labor union representative spoke. The public relations team laughed lightly.

"I appreciate you voicing your opinions and the needs of our constituents," the Mayor said. "I'm actually about to address the protestors, and I'll make sure to bring up those points because I know how imperative they are for the success of our city."

The labor union representative spoke again. The Mayor took a drink from his coffee mug, and then flicked the miniature pendulum on his desk, partially from boredom, and partially from anxiety.

"Well, sir," the Mayor said, "I hear you. And just know that the City of Portland is on the side of the working class. I apologize, but I do have to cut this short; the folks outside are waiting for a speech. I would encourage you to tune in, and I would love any feedback you have regarding our commitment to supporting all of Portland's people."

The Mayor hung up the phone and received a thumbs-up from the public relations specialist. He grabbed his speech paper from his speechwriter and scanned the revised version quickly.

"Well, we'd better get you out there," the public relations specialist said. "Remember, these people don't care about a plan; they just want to feel heard."

The Mayor nodded, took a deep breath, and strolled through the City Hall corridor. He pushed open the front doors of the building with power and forced kindness. As he approached the podium, streaks of sunshine peaked through the overcast sky; he heard a mixture of cheers and jeers. The Mayor set his speech down on the podium and addressed the crowd, and the cameras, with a well-rehearsed expression of empathy.

"Hello, my fellow Portlanders," the Mayor said. "As Mayor of this incredible city, I want to thank you for being here today to share your thoughts. Your presence here today demonstrates one of America's greatest liberties: the right to speak freely."

Garrett scanned the crowd to gauge the impact of his opening remarks. He spotted a protester near the front of the mob that was dressed like Rosie the Riveter. Garrett resisted the urge to laugh in mockery of the costume. He took a breath away from the microphone and continued his speech, looking directly into the news cameras.

"I want you to know that you are heard," the Mayor said. "I want you to know that your Mayor and your City have heard your call, and we intend to answer. The City of Portland is committed to all of you who are so essential for our success. Without our bus drivers, waiters, office workers, construction workers, and maintenance employees, our fine city would not stand. It is imperative that we draft and pass legislation that finally gives you hardworking Portlanders the respect you deserve. For too long, we've stood by and watched as prices have increased, while your wages have not. It's time to make a change. It's time to show the people of Portland that we all matter; we all deserve the same respect that we show our city. The City of Portland stands behind those who make our city the best in the world. Thank you all for coming out here to City Hall today to let your voices be heard. Know that your voices fall on compassionate and empathetic ears, and know that you are respected. Thank you."

The crowd of protestors erupted with cheers and claps. The Mayor smiled and waved. He pointed at a few random protestors as a strategy for showing personal connection; he knew the news would cast that scene as b-roll. When the applause died down, the Mayor gave one final wave, turned, and walked back into the building. When he returned to his office, his speechwriter and public relations specialist were waiting for him.

"Well done, Mr. Mayor."

THE PROTESTER

Rebecca raised her sign high above the crowd as she marched toward City Hall. She was particularly proud of her sign's clever slogan, especially compared to the blunt, heavy-handed statements she had seen on other signs as the morning moved forward.

The crowd began to pinch; Rebecca saw her girlfriend absorbed into another pocket of open space, so she pushed her way forward to stand beside her again.

"Ellen, I almost lost you," Rebecca said.

She smiled and grabbed Rebecca's free hand.

"Well, I'm glad you found me again," Ellen said.

As the crowd turned the corner, Rebecca saw City Hall rise above the city's greenery. The building hid in the shadows cast by the cloudy sky; the ground was wet with morning mist that had only begun to fade.

Stopping in front of City Hall, the protest leaders called

out choreographed chants on their megaphones, which riled the mob to respond with passion. Rebecca and Ellen rolled to a stop, taking turns holding their sign in support of the cause.

Rebecca, who graduated from Portland College two years ago, found a job as a server at a restaurant on 23rd. Though she collected a fair amount of money in tips on busy Saturday nights, she worked for minimum wage. With the rising cost of rent in her compact downtown apartment, she felt the need to find an additional serving job at another restaurant just to afford groceries. Luckily, Ellen moved in with her a few months earlier, which helped with the cost of rent.

When Rebecca was leaving work one evening, she noticed a pink flier posted on a wooden telephone pole that advertised a march to increase and equalize wages for all workers in the city. This was a cause she had to support.

As the day of the march drew closer, she began discussing it with some of her coworkers. Through these conversations, she realized that some of her male counterparts were, in fact, making more money than her female coworkers for doing the same work, even though most of the men had equal or lesser qualifications. She stomped home furiously and flung the apartment door open and fumed to Ellen about the injustices she was just beginning to recognize.

Sparking a fire in her studious brain, Ellen began researching the statistics on wage as it related to gender inequality, and her findings brought more fury to the apartment's conversation. Even at the higher levels of business, female executives made dramatically less money than their male counterparts, and for what reason? The prospect of pregnancy? Long-held stereotypes that perpetuated a patriarchal society? And why had no one ever mentioned the seriousness of this inequality to them before? School would have been a good place to start.

Rebecca and Ellen knew they had to march with a purpose. Of course, Rebecca wanted to raise the minimum wage, but more importantly, she wanted to bring attention to the issue of gender inequality. With a clever sign and a fiery spirit, she knew that this protest would bring the Mayor's attention to this issue.

When they arrived at the gathering point for the march, Rebecca looked around for people she may know, people who were in favor of increasing the standard of living for Portlanders, people who cared about fairness and justice. Men even carried signs advocating for women's income equality.

She was surprised, however, to see so many people who had purposefully obscured their identities. Marchers wore bandanas around their faces and masks that represented anarchical symbols. Why would these people be ashamed or embarrassed to march for such a just cause? Rebecca had never felt the inclination to do something as drastic as march for a cause before now, but she felt empowered and inspired.

As their march stopped in front of City Hall, Rebecca began to understand the desire for privacy within a march. Photographers, news cameras, and phones captured the event from every angle. Maybe some of these people did not want to be caught on the news marching for a cause they would not outwardly support otherwise.

The march leaders clearly did not care if they were photographed or caught on camera. They stood on platforms and hung on street light posts, calling to the crowd over megaphones. Their voices reverberated between buildings, picking up energy as the protestors echoed their calls.

Fair play! Equal pay!

We are going to win the day!

Fair play! Equal pay!

We are going to win the day!

The calls echoed as the crowd's pent-up emotions continued to rise. Police officers in tactical uniforms began to congregate around City Hall's front entrance; some moved forward with riot shields to scare potentially rambunctious protestors.

We're enraged! Raise the wage!

We're enraged! Raise the wage!

A few masked protestors moved in front of the chant leaders. As they began to move up the steps toward City Hall's front door, riot police moved toward them with shields, clubs, and force. Sensing a clash, the protest leaders called on the microphone for the masked rioters to back away and remain peaceful. They complied for the time being.

Rebecca squeezed Ellen's hand tightly. She smiled with emboldened enthusiasm as she caught Ellen's eye. Then, just when Rebecca thought the crowd couldn't shout any louder, the mob erupted with a mixture of cheers and jeers. Rebecca stood on her toes to see the cause of the commotion: the Mayor was walking toward the podium.

The sun cracked through the clouds, shining a natural spotlight on the Mayor as he waved to the crowd. He stepped to the podium with a swagger of a rising politician, an aura of smugness that Rebecca immediately disliked.

"Hello, my fellow Portlanders," the Mayor said. "As Mayor of this incredible city, I want to thank you for being here today to share your thoughts. Your presence here today demonstrates one of America's greatest liberties: the right to speak freely."

Rebecca looked at Ellen with a smirk, which Ellen returned. In their research about Portland's minimum wage and equal pay history, they discovered the Mayor's policies about the issues they were currently protesting, and he had not acted in accordance with the way he spoke. He had written policies that kept the minimum wage low, he was financed by big businesses who made large profits by exploiting large amounts of minimum wage workers, and he did this all while claiming to be a leader of the people.

"This guy is a liar," Rebecca said. "He's going to stand up there and say he's a champion for the people, that he's one of us. But he's not. He's a crook."

Rebecca jumped up onto the curb for a better view, though she could hear the speech just fine. As she climbed the curb, Ellen followed her closely. They made their way closer to the podium so they could participate in the cheering and jeering of the Mayor's upcoming remarks.

"I want you to know that you are heard," the Mayor said. "I want you to know that your Mayor and your City have heard your call, and we intend to answer. The City of Portland is committed to all of you who are so essential for our success. Without our bus drivers, waiters..."

Rebecca stopped listening. She knew this was all political theater. He was telling the crowd what they wanted to hear, just like politicians always did. The crowd would eat this up, the Mayor would gain more support from the people, and then he would return to his office and craft policies that repaid the big businesses that financed his re-election campaign. That's how it always happened.

The crowd of protestors erupted with cheers and claps. The Mayor smiled and waved. Then, he caught Rebecca's eye and pointed directly at her, expecting to draw her in as another supporter. Or maybe he just wanted himself to look good on camera; the same cameras that captured the protestors were also focusing on the Mayor's reaction.

When the applause died down, the Mayor gave one final wave, turned, and walked back into the building, where, Rebecca assumed, he would move away from the protestors' demands and return to business as usual.

Rebecca felt deflated. She pulled Ellen's hand as they moved against the stream of the crowd to leave the protest. She wanted to go home. Rebecca dropped her sign on the concrete, a casualty of the day's events.

"What was the point of all this?" Rebecca asked, fighting back tears.

"What do you mean?" Ellen said. "We were *heard*. The Mayor acknowledged our demands."

Rebecca subconsciously shouldered a protester out of the way; anger swirled with deflation.

"No he didn't," Rebecca said. "He just told us what we wanted to hear. No action will come from this. This is how it always happens."

They walked silently through the Park Blocks; the cheers and chants of the protestors faded to a quiet echo.

THE ATHLETE

The sun twinkled on 12th Avenue. A light rain shower had finally dispelled, giving way to cool, summer sunshine that reflected off every droplet that clung to street signs and windows. The sun caused evaporation, bringing with it a feeling of humidity, but without that drastic heat that accompanied southern humidity. Marcus enjoyed that feeling; it reminded him of home, only a bit more pleasant. But he was still a long way from Kentucky.

After his third day in Portland, Marcus was becoming more familiar with the city already, at least the downtown area. He had ventured into Southeast once, but just to get his haircut, which didn't turn out like he had hoped. The white barber messed up his fade a little.

He knew that people in Portland were friendly, for the most part. The homeless people that camped in doorways and underneath bridges seemed a little scary at first, but since no one else seemed to mind, he decided not to mind either. And the protest the other day was a little much. Marcus wasn't entirely sure what its purpose was, but it sure drew a lot of people.

He moved down 12th with confidence, a certain swagger that grew more apparent with each step. Yet, his confidence was slightly exaggerated to mask a feeling of nervousness. He didn't know anybody in the city, not even a single teammate. He didn't know where to go, where to eat, or where to hang out.

And then there was the nervousness that came with being a rookie in the league.

Drafted by the Trail Blazers out of his junior year in college, Marcus knew that making the jump to professional basketball would be difficult. He knew that his teammates had been in the league for a long time and they knew the ropes. They knew each other. They didn't know him.

His legs ached from a hard morning workout: squats, box jumps, sprints, and jump rope, followed by a one-on-one technical training session with a team assistant coach. Official team practices didn't start for another month or so, but Marcus wanted to be ready. He wanted to make an early impression.

But he also didn't want to burn himself out too early; the season was a long one, and he hoped to see some significant playing time. Ideally, he would work his way into the starting lineup. He hoped to be in Portland for a while. At least through the duration of his initial contract.

He wanted to familiarize himself with the city, so he

decided to explore. Maybe treat himself to a calorie-filled meal. He was young; his body could handle it.

Marcus approached the restaurant, a burger spot that someone at his new barbershop recommended. As he strolled across the street, people gawked at him. He was used to this by now; as a 6-foot-9 guy, everyone just assumed he was a famous basketball player. In Kentucky, he certainly was; everyone in the state recognized him. But in a new city, he wasn't quite sure how people would react yet.

"How many are in your party today?" the hostess asked Marcus.

"Just me," he replied.

The hostess hid a smile by grabbing a menu.

"I'd love to sit outside if there's something available," Marcus said. "I'm new here and I want to take in the city, you know?"

"Right this way," the hostess said.

She led Marcus through a bustling, renovated building that once served as a warehouse. Old steel beams and exposed brick adorned the interior. A trendy bar filled the middle of the floor; two big screen televisions hung from the walls. Two guys sat at the bar, clearly in a heated discussion about something trivial. A few business meetings took place over lunch throughout the restaurant floor. The interior was dark, made for nightlife. But on a day like this, Marcus wanted to be outside.

He followed the hostess through the door and to his outdoor table, which sat atop an old loading dock perched just above the sidewalk. Rows of old loading docks lined the street as far as Marcus could see. The street used to house warehouses and factories. Decades ago, no one would have come to 12th Avenue for fun, just to clock in.

"Is this table alright, sir?" the hostess asked.

"This is perfect," Marcus said. "Thank you."

The hostess walked away with a forced calm, stealing backwards glances at Marcus as she returned indoors. The waitress appeared moments later with a glass of water.

"Can I get you started with something?" the server asked.

"Just a coffee, please," Marcus said.

A family with two kids sat at a table adjacent to Marcus. The young boy looked at Marcus with intent. It took a minute for the dad to notice before he corrected him and told him that it was not polite to stare. Marcus smiled, assuming the boy knew that he played for the Blazers.

Marcus had noticed quite a bit of citywide pride for their basketball franchise. He knew that Portland was a smaller market, especially compared to cities like New York and Los Angeles, but he was fine with that. Portland had a limited number of professional sports teams, so he assumed that he could make a major impact on the city as one of its only soon-to-be star athletes. Hopefully he could positively impact kids, like the one who was sitting across from him, the one who continued to steal glances when his dad wasn't looking.

As Marcus drank his coffee, he sketched out a rough financial plan. He had a meeting with his financial advisor in a few days, but he wanted to enter that meeting with a clear picture of his long-term goals. He knew that he needed to save a large majority of his salary; ideally, he wanted to invest much of that savings in low-risk funds that would accrue interest over time. He knew that there was a lot of pressure in league culture to spend, spend, spend. As much as he told himself that he wouldn't fall into that trap of buying houses, cars, shoes, clothes, and lavish dinners, he had to plan for that as well. And, though endorsement deals would come, he didn't have any yet, so he needed to craft his budget around his league salary. Which, by comparison to any other job in the world, was ridiculous.

Marcus was quite savvy when it came to mathematics. He achieved high scores in AP Calculus in high school, and he enjoyed his college statistics class. He had played the stock market since he was in middle school, an interest that had actually made him a decent sum of money for someone his age. As Marcus sketched out the blueprint for his financial success, he saw a person appear in his peripheral vision. The little boy from the adjacent table stood politely next to Marcus.

"Excuse me, sir," the boy said.

"Hey, what's up, little man?" Marcus said.

"Do you play for the Blazers?" the boy said.

Marcus noticed the boy's dad, who watched the conversation nervously from his seat at the family's table.

"Yes I do," Marcus said. "Are you a basketball fan?"

"Yes I am," the boy said timidly.

Marcus smiled, and dropped his shoulders further to the boy's level.

"That's cool," Marcus said.

He paused and glanced at the dad again; a smile began to

emerge.

"Hey, buddy," Marcus said. "Would you like an autograph?"

The boy smiled, showing his four missing teeth.

"Yes, please," the boy said, trying to suppress his wild excitement.

The boy pulled a napkin from his pocket in hopes that Marcus would sign it. Marcus had a better idea. He reached into his backpack and pulled out a white headband that he received as part of a welcome package from the team. He signed it, handed it to the boy, and shook his hand.

"What's your name, little man?" Marcus asked.

"Stevie," the boy said.

"Stevie, it's nice to meet you," he said. "I'm Marcus Jones."

"I know," Stevie said. "I watched every minute of the draft with my dad. We're excited that you're in Portland, and not someplace else."

"Well, thank you, Stevie," Marcus said. "It was very nice to meet you."

Marcus looked at the boy's dad again, who nodded in honest appreciation. Marcus leaned back in his chair, smiled, and sipped his coffee.

THE FAN

The bartender poured beer into two pint glasses from the tap. She waited for a bit of excess foam to subside, an uncharacteristically lazy pour. She placed both beers in front of the two guys sitting at the bar. They were enthralled by whatever the sportscaster was discussing on the television screen above her head. Luckily, there was closed captioning, so she didn't have to listen to that boring sports talk.

Jimmy snatched his beer as soon as it hit the bar top. He took a sip of his favorite IPA and wiped the foam from his moustache. His white hand contrasted with the beer's dark brown shade. Andre methodically grabbed his pilsner and took a drink, gasping inaudibly from its crisp, refreshing nature, his black hand converse to the pale pilsner.

"You get a haircut?" Jimmy asked.

"Yeah, man," Andre said.

"You went with the fade this time instead of your usual

mohawk?" Jimmy said.

Andre smiled.

"Yeah, now that I'm a banker, I'm trying out a more professional look," Andre said.

Jimmy rolled his eyes.

"So, you're telling me that Fun Andre is a thing of the past, huh?" Jimmy said.

"No, I'll always be Fun Andre," he said, "but I'm growing up a little."

They smiled and both took drinks of their beers. Andre looked up at the television screen, subconsciously encouraging Jimmy to do the same.

"Here we go," Jimmy said, nodding toward the television screen. "All they'll be talking about until the season starts are the draft picks and who's going to contribute."

"At least the Blazers picked some solid guys," Andre said.

Jimmy thought about the team's picks with a focus that most people only dedicate to a dense novel. His pale knuckles turned whiter as he clasped his hands together.

"I still can't believe they didn't pick Smith out of Duke," Jimmy said. "He was the best center in the draft, and they don't have a big man."

"But Davis is so shifty," Andre said. "We need a shooting guard to take pressure off the point. I'm glad we took him instead."

The bartender eavesdropped on the conversation. She enjoyed collecting her customers' perspectives on sports; it helped her with small talk later on in the evening, which also helped with tip money.

The television screen scrolled through the draft selections that occurred just last month. Commentators played their *I Told You So* cards, demonstrating their superior abilities to analyze teams and organizational needs. Funny how they only mentioned the predictions they guessed correctly, ignoring their missteps.

"What do you think about Jones?" Jimmy asked.

"Marcus Jones?" Andre said. "He's the truth. A smooth, tall forward who can get rebounds, but also pull up from three. He's just an all-around athlete."

"Yeah, but I think there were better players ahead of him that we should have taken," Jimmy said.

Andre's face scrunched and he raised a condescending eyebrow at his friend.

"Like who?" Andre said.

"Well, Jamison out of Notre Dame," Jimmy said. "He's a true center. Big guy, almost seven feet. We could use a guy like that in the middle."

"That goofy white guy who can't shoot, dribble, *or* pass?" Andre said. "I'm glad we stayed away from him."

The bartender turned her face away from the customers and laughed as she pretended to clean a pint glass.

"I don't know, man," Jimmy said. "I just don't think Marcus Jones will contribute much to the team."

Andre raised another eyebrow at his friend, who sipped his beer as he planned his justification statement for his last opinion.

"Did you see him in the tournament?" Jimmy said. "He looked so lazy. Plus, I heard he lacked some work ethic in the classroom at Kentucky."

Andre waved him off and took a drink of his beer.

"Man, that's all rumors," Andre said. "The kid decided to *stay* at Kentucky and finish his degree, which he was able to finish early because he took such a dense course load. He could have jumped into the league two years ago, but he wanted to finish his education. That's some character right there."

Jimmy slouched his shoulders, signifying his defeat in the argument. He raised a hand to get the bartender's attention. She walked over to the guys, who asked for another round of drinks.

As she placed the new, full pint glasses in front of them on the bar top, the restaurant door opened. The glass door reflected emerging sunlight across the room, forcing Jimmy and Andre to look up. As they did, they saw a tall man walk through the room. Andre looked at Jimmy with wide eyes, nearly dropping his full beer in the process.

"That's Marcus Jones," Andre whispered.

"Sure is," Jimmy said.

"That's the future right there, Jimmy," Andre said.

He put his beer down on the bar top.

"I'm going to go talk to him," Jimmy said.

Andre stuck his arm out to stop him.

"Man, don't bother the guy," Andre said. "He just wants to eat some lunch. Let him eat in peace, and maybe we'll catch him on his way out."

Jimmy returned to a stable, seated position, grabbing his pint glass to solidify his place at the bar.

"Plus, you don't even like the guy," Andre said, smirking.

"Shut up, man," Jimmy said. "I never said that. I just had my doubts."

They watched as Jones strolled through the restaurant with confidence, looking like he owned the place. The hostess looked tiny compared to him. She opened the door that led to the outdoor patio, and he followed, taking a seat by himself. Andre and Jimmy could just see him through the large glass window as he investigated his street view from his table. They saw a young family at an adjacent table notice Jones, too. The dad's eyes grew wide, and one of the kids begged his dad to go over and talk to him.

The bartender laughed at the two guys; their attention completely diverted from the television to the athlete.

Even though the guys had only planned on grabbing a few beers, they decided to stay for lunch. Though neither of them overtly said it, they wanted to extend their time at the bar in hopes of running into Marcus Jones. The bartender brought out sandwiches and fries, which they ate slowly, strategically.

After what seemed like hours, Andre saw Jones receive his bill. He stood and strolled through the restaurant again. Jimmy was stuck, too nervous to make a move. Andre stood and walked into the walkway to meet him.

"Hey, you're Marcus Jones, right?" Andre asked.

"Yeah, man," Jones said.

"Cool, cool, "Andre said. "Hey, man, we're glad to have you here in our city. You're a phenomenal ball player, and you seem like a good dude."

"Thanks, man," Jones said. "I appreciate the love. I'm just

excited to be here."

They shook hands genuinely. Jones turned to walk away, but then he turned back toward Andre with a serious expression.

"Hey, man, can I ask you something?" Jones asked.

Andre nodded.

"Where'd you get your haircut?"

THE RUNNER

Puddles stood like obstacles on the pavement. Leftovers from the morning rain. Mark didn't mind. In fact, he enjoyed it. Each time his stride led him to a standing pool of water, he planted his foot with purpose, affirming his ability to conquer the elements.

That's what running was about for Mark. He ran to prove to himself that he could. No one else. Just himself. He still had that competitive edge, that uncanny desire to push his body further than the average human body could go.

Sure, he followed other sports. He was excited about the Blazers' draft class, and he followed Portland's soccer teams religiously. But running was personal. He competed with himself, and there was always competition.

But that true competitive stage in his running career had long since passed him by. At 45, Mark was no longer a competitive runner, at least not in the same capacity that he was when he ran long distance in college. Those were the days.

He used to wake up before sunrise, lace up his featherlight, durable training shoes, and run a casual six miles before coming back to his house to get ready for class. Between classes, he might put some middle-distance sprints on the track, just to train for that final push. He also liked to look at the stands at Hayward Field as he ran. He envisioned thousands of fans cheering for him as he made that final lap at the NCAA Finals. Before bed, he might put in a few more miles in the hills, maybe near Pre's Rock, just to pay homage to the legend that helped build Tracktown, USA.

Mark didn't run this much because he wanted to become an Olympian, or even a national champion, although those would have been added benefits. He ran this much to be free. Free from a schedule. Free from the world's problems. Even free from his own problems. When he was running, that's all he was doing: running.

Now, Mark woke up each morning before work, before his desk job, to put in three miles or so. He had to. It was as if his self-worth was tied to his ability to run a passable mile time. But that time was waning; his knees were starting to give out. After putting so many miles on those knees over the last three decades, the cartilage was starting to erode, and Mark could feel it with every step.

The rain started to pick up again. Just a drizzle, though. A typical Portland morning drizzle. Mark was used to running in the chilly, misty air. He thrived on it. He focused on breathing in the clean air from the evergreen trees that surrounded the streets in Southeast Portland. He smelled the pine. He breathed in the distinct aroma of rain hitting concrete, a smell that only a true Portlander could love.

As he turned the corner, Mark saw a pair of runners coming in his direction. A couple, most likely. He smiled casually and said "Good morning" as they passed, a phrase that he timed perfectly with his naturally-paced exhale. He turned and saw the couple continue their casual run; he shook his head and laughed. Mark never understood running with a partner, unless they were true long-distance training partners. The point of running was to push yourself, and he never understood how running with someone else allowed a person to honestly push themselves. Either you were concerned that you were running too fast for that person, so you slowed down, or you were concerned that the other person was slowing their pace for you, so you outran a smart pace in order to prove your worth, ultimately sacrificing an intelligent pace in the end.

Mark pushed through the thought and rounded the corner on his return leg of his usual route. He was catching a solo runner. Mark liked to make noise as he approached a runner from behind, just to let them know he was coming. Sometimes he would cough, or slam his feet loudly. As he approached the runner, he saw that the man was wearing headphones; the guy wouldn't hear Mark approaching anyway, so what was the point? He never understood running with headphones. Why did a real runner need another person singing at them in order to motivate their speed? A person should be able to push their limits without the motivation of an external force.

The runner seemed to slow as the rain picked up; Mark's competitive training kicked in and he increased the length of his stride. He flew by the solo jogger, a man that Mark could tell was new to running. He must have been sticking to his New Year's Resolution or something. But he was running all wrong. His elbows stuck out. His head moved too far from one side to the other. And his stride was short and forced.

As Mark made a left into an isolated forest path, he finally felt his competitive sentiments subside. He enjoyed running in the woods, especially this path. He had never seen a single person running on this path, at least not this early in the morning. He appreciated the solitude that this path brought, the peace and tranquility that he found while running through the city's forests. He also enjoyed the incline that Mt. Tabor brought to his regular morning loop. Mark loved the idea that he was running in a forest at the base of a dormant volcano. Sometimes, he envisioned that the volcano erupted, and he had to outrun the volcano's blast in order to survive.

Exiting the forest, Mark knew that his daily ritual was nearly complete. He saw his house down the block, and he slowed his jog as he approached. He loved his morning runs. They brought peace, solitude, and introspection to his day. In hindsight, that's why he ran so much in college; he loved the alone time. The time to think. The time to *be*.

He showered, put on his shirt and tie, and slunk into his sedan. With talk radio murmuring over his speakers, he knew that the best part of his day was over, the only time he could really be himself, the only time he could really think.

His cubicle was monotonous. A few pictures of family, a calendar, and a decade-old desktop computer. Mark opened his regular computer programs, shifted some numbers and data, and made small talk with coworkers and acquaintances in the common area. The same routine happened last week, and the week before, and the year before that. And the same routine would happen for the next ten years.

When lunchtime approached, Mark opened his briefcase and reached for his leftovers. He frequently hoped that one day, he would find his running shoes in his briefcase. He would look around his office and all of the people glued to their screens and paperwork in their little cubicles. He would forget about the piles of paperwork on his own desk in his own monotonous cubicle. He would take his shoes out of his briefcase. He would put them on, lace them up, and run out the door. Finally, free again.

THE SINGLE FATHER

Samir woke groggily. His alarm blared on his bedside table; he punched it to turn off the noise. He looked at his alarm clock: 5:15 a.m. Another Wednesday morning.

He stuffed his face into his pillow, fighting the urge to go back to sleep. It hadn't been a late night, just another rendition of a classic animated movie and some popcorn, but the weekday grind was getting to him.

Throwing his covers off the side of the bed, Samir stood and yawned before making his way to the bathroom to brush his teeth. He remembered when he used to wake up early and go running, but those days of personal motivation were far in the past.

He showered, and then put on his usual shirt and tie combination before walking into the kitchen. He grabbed three brown paper bags and placed them on the counter. Diving into the refrigerator, he snagged some ham, cheese, and lettuce. He efficiently made three sandwiches and tossed them in their respective lunch bags. Then, he added three ready-to-go yogurts, along with apples, chips, and juice boxes.

With lunches made, he walked outside to grab the newspaper. Though the sun was beginning to rise, the overcast gloom kept the Southeast Portland sky dark. Samir looked down the alleyway at a few other houses, feeling like he was the only house who still received the morning paper.

As he walked inside, he heard a door creak down the hallway. Thinking nothing of it, he sat in his customary wooden chair at the head of the kitchen table and cracked open the newspaper. The front-page story featured a prominent local shoe company that had sponsored the construction of a new high school gym.

Finally, some positive news, Samir thought.

He heard the shower turn on in the hallway bathroom. Checking his watch, he knew that the morning routine was already off to a slow start. Another door creaked down the hallway, followed by groggy footsteps. A middle school girl lumbered into the kitchen wearing sweatpants and a baggy sweatshirt. Her black curly hair puffed out around her head.

"Good morning, Maggie," Samir said in an overtly chipper tone.

"Uh huh, "Maggie said, rolling her eyes as she rubbed the sleep out of them.

Samir smiled. *Ah, teenage angst*, he thought.

"You're up a little late," Samir said. "Did you stay up too late finishing your homework?"

"Ugh, yeah," Maggie said. "Mr. Harper assigned a five-paragraph essay with the most complicated prompt ever."

"Did he assign it yesterday?" Samir asked.

"Well, not exactly," Maggie said. "He assigned it, like, last week, but…"

"Maybe next time you could get a jump on your homework, Maggie, dearest," Samir said with a sly smile.

Maggie rolled her eyes and smirked back as she grabbed the cereal box from the cupboard. Samir pulled the sports section from the newspaper and slid it across the table to Maggie's usual spot. She plopped her cereal bowl on the table and flipped the newspaper open.

"Is your sister going to be in the shower all day?" Samir said. "She's running late already."

Maggie laughed and looked up from the article she was ready.

"Dad, now that Aisha is in high school, she's been taking such long showers, walkin' around here like she owns the place."

Samir laughed and took a drink of his coffee.

"Will you go bang on the door and tell her to hurry up?" Samir asked. "And then can you make sure your little sister is awake, please?"

Maggie rolled her eyes and closed the newspaper dramatically before standing to follow her orders.

Three girls and one bathroom in the house, Samir thought, shaking his head and returning to the newspaper.

Maggie banged on the bathroom door and yelled at Aisha to hurry up. Then, she moved down the hallway to Kira's door, throwing it open with the absolute authority granted by her father.

"Wake up, Kira!" Maggie shouted, flickering the lights on and off.

Kira buried herself in her sheets, feeling startled and jarred by the light and loud noises. Her petite elementary school frame made her almost blend in with her fluffy comforter and absurd number of pillows.

"Maggie, why do you always have to do that?" Kira shouted, muffled by the comforter.

"Dad told me to," Maggie said. "Time to get up."

Maggie returned to her spot at the table and buried herself in the newspaper again. Kira stumbled out of her room and joined the family at the kitchen table with her cereal bowl.

"Good morning, Sweetie," Samir said.

"Good morning, Daddy," Kira said.

"How'd you sleep?" Samir asked.

"Fine," Kira said. "I just really didn't want to get out of bed this morning. Why does fourth grade have to start so early?"

Samir threw his head back dramatically and laughed.

The bathroom door opened and Aisha walked down the hallway and into the kitchen. Her hair was freshly braided, a stark contrast to the puffy bedhead exhibited by Maggie and Kira.

"Well good morning, Sunshine," Samir said.

"Good morning," Aisha said. "And actually, the sun isn't even up yet."

Samir caught Maggie's attention and they both rolled their eyes and laughed.

"Daddy," Kira said, "Can you braid my hair like Aisha's?"

"Kira, I wish I could, but I'm just not that good at braiding," Samir said. "Mommy used to do all the braiding."

A sad smile crossed his face. The car accident replayed in his mind, just like it did every time he mentioned his wife.

"Kira," Aisha said. "She taught me how to braid. I can do it."

Aisha looked at Maggie, and both of their eyes lowered to mask the longing they had for their mother.

The blue car weaved through the Southeast Portland side streets. Samir liked to avoid the major thoroughfares during rush hour. He nodded his head to the beat of hip-hop music that came from the car speakers. Aisha sat up front; she always chose the music. Kira and Maggie sat in the back. Maggie shook her head at her father's attempts to groove to the modern music. She and Aisha laughed at him almost every morning.

The car pulled into the elementary school parking lot. Samir followed the organized traffic routine, which was orchestrated efficiently by the fifth-grade safety patrol and supervised by the Parent-Teacher Organization volunteers. Kira jumped out of the car with her backpack. Samir put the car in park and jumped out, too.

"Have a great day, Sweetie," Samir said. "I'll see you after school. Love you."

Kira turned and sprinted to the front doors.

"Her dad is doing so well," a mom said.

"He's here every morning and every afternoon," another

mom said.

"I know," said the first mom. "And to do that all with three girls. Good for him."

The blue car slowly rolled through the elementary school traffic route before moving on to Aisha's high school parking lot just a few blocks away. Aisha turned her music up just a little before exiting the car, just to give Maggie something to jam to.

"Have a great day, Girlie," Samir said.

"Love you, Dad," Aisha said as she hopped out of the car.

Samir smiled and looked at Maggie through the rear view mirror.

"You hear that?" Samir said. "Even though she's a big, bad high schooler now, she still tells me that she loves me."

"Well of course she does," Maggie said. "I mean, you are our *Dad*."

Samir smiled widely. The blue car pulled onto the street and made its way to the next stop of the morning.

THE LITTLE GIRL

Amelia pulled her hair back into a tight ponytail and fastened her bike helmet underneath her chin. She whipped her bike around the garage clutter, corralling it outside onto the driveway. She stood nervously on the cement, gripping the handlebars, trying not to talk herself out of it. Looking over her shoulder, she saw her dad wave to her with an encouraging smile. She couldn't turn back now.

She looked at her bike. Silver with purple accents. Ten speeds, which she had mastered during countless rides around her Northeast Portland neighborhood. Her parents only let her stay between 20th and 30th, and Skidmore and Alameda. The front of her bike had a basket. She planned to carry her backpack in the basket when she rode her bike to school this coming year after summer ended (she didn't want summer to end, but she *was* excited to start third grade).

Loud voices echoed down the street. They seemed to

move closer to Amelia's house. Then, she heard the sound of bicycles racing at top speed. The boys came dashing around the corner and whizzed by Amelia's driveway. But then, Bobby and Jamal screeched to a stop and returned to talk to Amelia.

"Hey!" Bobby shouted. "Come ride with us."

Amelia hesitated. She looked at her feet.

"Where are you going to ride?" she asked.

"I think we're going to Deadman's Hill," Jamal said.

Amelia's heart began to race. Her eyes widened. Panic began to overtake her nerves.

"My parents won't let me," Amelia said honestly.

Bobby and Jamal laughed. Amelia's face turned bright red and she started to feel angry, though she wasn't sure who her anger was directed toward.

"You don't have to ride *down* Deadman's Hill," Bobby said. "We know it's probably too scary for you anyway."

Amelia gritted her teeth and clenched her handlebars.

"Alright, I'll come with you," she said, "but I'm not going to ride down the hill. Not because I'm scared, but just because my parents won't let me."

Bobby smiled condescendingly. He hopped back on his bike and started to speed away. Jamal followed. Amelia jumped on her bike and pedaled hard to keep up.

Deadman's Hill was only a few blocks away, but the ride seemed unending. The sun beat down on the concrete, producing a humid heat that drained Amelia's energy quicker than usual. Her blonde hair darkened as she began to perspire.

As she pedaled toward Bobby, she noticed his bike getting closer, which meant she was catching up. She pedaled with more force, more motivation.

Bobby and Jamal were the coolest kids in school. They were strong, athletic, good-looking kids. Bobby was the best football player at recess, and Jamal was definitely the best soccer player. And they were both wicked smart. Amelia knew that they were becoming too cool for her, but she had been neighbors with both boys since she was born. But they were starting to become kind of mean. She sometimes felt like they were just bringing her along so they could be better than her at things.

As she rounded the corner of Alameda, she saw Bobby and Jamal stop. The street narrowed. Trees created a darkened archway. There it was. Deadman's Hill.

Deadman's Hill was the steepest hill in the neighborhood. It was so steep that cars weren't even allowed to drive up it. Creepy old staircases jutted out from it so pedestrians didn't have to strain themselves with its decline. The curbs still had metal loops that early Portlanders used to tie up their horses.

Amelia pulled her bike alongside Jamal's and looked down. The hill seemed to go on for miles, ending in a six-way intersection. A shiver crept up her spine and into her neck.

"Alright, who's first?" Jamal asked.

Bobby looked around at the trees like he didn't hear the question.

"Hey, why is it called Deadman's Hill, anyway?" Bobby asked.

"You don't know the legends?" Jamal said.

Amelia and Bobby both shook their heads. Jamal settled into his bike seat and nodded his head, pushing his glasses down, giving him an aura of wisdom. He cleared his throat methodically.

"A hundred years ago," Jamal said, "a thief robbed the old mansion down the block. He was speeding along the road on his horse. This very road. When he reached this hill here, his horse pulled up to a stop, too afraid to go down it. But the thief was determined, so he forced his horse to charge full speed. Halfway down the hill, a tree branch caught the thief in the neck, stopping his body on the branch. The horse kept going, never to be heard from again. When the authorities arrived, the man's body was hanging from the tree, like a hangman's noose"

Amelia and Bobby looked wide-eyed at Jamal's tale.

"To this day," Jamal continued, "the ghost of the thief haunts this very hill. As penance, he protects those who are deemed worthy to pass, and he offers no protection to those who are not."

Amelia gripped her handlebars; her knuckles turned white with fear. Bobby's knuckles did the same, but Amelia didn't notice.

Jamal returned his glasses to their original position, and his expression of sage wisdom had vanished, leaving only the contented smile of a successful storyteller.

"So, who's first," Jamal asked.

"You've both ridden your bikes down Deadman's Hill before, right?" Amelia asked.

Jamal and Bobby looked at each other with expressions of

false confidence.

"Uh, well, um," Bobby stammered.

"No, I haven't," Jamal said. "But I'm not scared to do it."

"I haven't either," Bobby said, "but not because I'm scared. I've just been waiting for the right time."

"So, why don't you go first?" Amelia asked Bobby.

Bobby laughed, hiding his fear.

"You need to go first," Bobby said. "We know we're both going to do it. We want to make sure you don't chicken out like a little girl."

Amelia's eyes flitted with anger. She wrung her hands along her handlebars and secured her stance on her bike.

"Oh yeah?" she shouted. "I'll show you what little girls can do."

Amelia slammed her right foot down on her pedal, shifting gears as she charged forward. She stopped her pedaling and began to glide, balancing her feet on both pedals as she lifted herself off of her seat. Deadman's Hill approached.

The front tire tipped over the decline; she was committed. Her momentum carried her forward even faster. Wind blew her ponytail behind her, and her eyes squinted. Adrenaline charged through her veins. She felt like she was flying.

As she charged to the midpoint of the hill, she noticed a tree branch above her. The wind made the leaves dance, as if they were waving to her. She smiled.

Amelia began to panic as the stop sign approached. The end of Deadman's Hill was getting closer. Too close. Too quickly. The crazy intersection was buzzing with cars.

After the stop sign, the hill immediately flattened out. Amelia slammed on her breaks and shifted her weight to one side. Her bike skidded to stop. *Style points*, she thought.

Amelia looked up the hill and waved to the boys, encouraging them to follow in her footsteps, in the trail she had just blazed. But when they didn't make a move to ride down the hill, she jumped off of her bike and walked it back up the same way she came. As she reached the top of the hill, she noticed Jamal and Bobby silently looking around, avoiding eye contact with her.

"What's the hold up?" Amelia asked. "Something wrong with your bikes?"

"Um, well," Jamal said, "I, I think I have to get home for lunch."

"Yeah, um, I, well," Bobby said.

Amelia smiled proudly.

"You chickens."

THE MECHANIC

The noise of power tools and engines filled the small shop. The metallic walls fluttered with the strobe of flying sparks. The large garage doors were open, allowing light mist to enter just inside the shop, dampening the cement floor. Cars rushed by on the bustling street outside as rush hour began to build.

Marley grabbed a wrench from her workbench. She looked at it, looked back at the sports car she was tuning, and grabbed a different wrench instead. She cranked her arm into a crevasse between the engine block and loosened a bolt, which released the clamp she was planning to adjust. After replacing the clamp with a new one, she tightened the bolt and closed the hood.

She sat on the plastic that covered the front seat, popped the clutch, and revved the engine. *That sounds beautiful*, she thought. After three days of tuning and adjusting this one-of-a-kind European sports car, she felt a sense of pride. A sense of victory.

Marley whipped the sports car into the parking lot like she used to do with her bike as a kid. She parked it next to a few other cars that her crew had finished tuning. She loved working on foreign cars. They were challenging. The run-of-the-mill sedans were too easy. When she saw the red, angular car pull into the shop a few days ago, she claimed it. She had the power to do that; after all, she was the lead mechanic.

Strolling effortlessly through the Portland rain, Marley walked back into the garage. She cleaned off some of her tools that had received some wear during the sports car job, and then she replaced them in their proper spot in her workbench. She grabbed a bad cup of coffee and moved into the front office to await the next customer.

Local sports scores from last night's high school football games scrolled across the television screen in the customer waiting room. She saw that Douglass High School had beaten Adams, which filled her with yet another sense of pride. Although she was seven years removed from graduation, she loved to see her old school succeed. After all, it was because of that school that she had found her passion.

Douglass High School featured a unique curriculum; it offered technical skills classes that allowed students to interact with certain trades. Marley remembered taking woodshop, metalshop, computer science, and her favorite, auto shop. She was placed in it randomly as a freshman. When she saw *auto shop* on her schedule, she was so upset, worrying that she would break a nail and have greasy hands and that the boys would make fun of her.

All of that happened. But so did something else: passion. As a freshman, Marley was able to solve auto mechanic issues that usually only seniors could tackle. In fact, her teacher had her schedule adjusted so she could take advance auto shop *with* seniors. She felt at home in that school auto shop. White students, black students, kids from Mexico, Somalia, Russia, and Syria. She even met a fellow Puerto Rican girl from the same town as Marley's parents. She learned more about language and culture in that class than in history and Spanish combined. And she made some genuine friends and acquired some positive role models.

As she strolled through the halls to math class with chipped fingernails and greased up palms each afternoon, she felt a sense of pride. Seniors would call out to her, a little freshman. The captain of the basketball team would hive-five her and call her *The Magician* every time he saw her, on account of her uncanny ability to solve problems in class. Marley's freshman friends were in awe of the upperclassmen she knew, and the level of respect they showed her.

By the time her senior year came around, she knew she didn't have the money to attend a four-year university. And she didn't want to. All she wanted to do was work on cars. She earned her associate's degree in two years, and then earned a spot on the mechanic team at her current shop by leveraging a former upperclassman from high school that remembered her skills as a freshman.

Marley snapped from her daze of memories as the bell rang. A customer powered through the door. The middle-aged man bustled his way to the front counter; his expensive suit filled him with a false sense of authority.

"I need my car fixed right now," he said to Marley.

She tried her best to hold a neutral expression in the face of such rudeness.

"Good morning, sir," Marley said. "What seems to be the issue with your car?"

"It's new, but for some reason, it's jerking every time I change gears," he said. "I didn't buy an expensive sports car for it to break down on me. I need one of those guys to fix it today."

Marley smiled. Secretly, she enjoyed when rich, powerful white guys came in and failed to recognize that they knew nothing about cars.

"I'd be happy to fix your car myself today, sir," she said.

"You?" the man said. "I'd prefer one of those guys in the garage fix it."

Marley grinned coyly. She wasn't surprised; men often dismissed her skill on account of her gender. She was used to handling situations like these in her field.

"As the leader of the mechanic team," Marley said, "I'd be happy to pass your car off to one of my less-experienced understudies, if that's what you would prefer."

The man subconsciously took a step back.

"You're the leader of the team?" he said. "Well, why don't you take a look and have one of your guys look at it too."

Marley resisted the temptation to punch him in his rich little nose.

"I'll pull your car into the garage and we'll take a look at it for you," she said.

With the green sports car in the garage, Marley looked under the hood. *Brand new*, she thought. *Perfect condition*. She lifted the car and rolled underneath it. The transmission looked new as well, aside from a few marks left by poor user gear shifting.

She smiled authoritatively. *This guy doesn't know how to drive a stick*, she thought.

"Hey, Deandre," Marley shouted to another mechanic nearby. "Roll up under here and tell me why this car isn't shifting properly."

Deandre knelt down and rolled underneath the car. After less than thirty seconds of investigation, he laughed. Loudly. His laugh boomed and echoed through the garage.

He emerged from underneath the car and caught his breath.

"Homie doesn't know how to drive a stick," Deandre said.

Marley smiled.

"That's what I was thinking, too," she said.

"Yo, Mario," Deandre said. "Look under here and tell us what's wrong with this transmission."

Mario raised an eyebrow, put his wrench down, and rolled underneath the car. Soon, his laugh was heard echoing through the garage too.

The rich man saw mechanics start to gather around his sports car through the garage window. He knew something major must be wrong with his brand new status symbol.

Marley, Deandre, and Mario walked across the garage and into the customer waiting room. Marley led the team, walking with confidence and humility. Deandre's dreadlocks swung from his shoulders. Mario hooked his thumbs on his belt loops. They smiled at each other; this was going to be a first for all three of them.

As they pushed through the door into the waiting room, the man looked at them with slight disdain and immense impatience.

"What's wrong with it?" the man demanded.

Deandre smiled. Mario held back a laugh.

"Well, sir," Marley said. "Let's start by suggesting some driving lessons."

THE RIVERBOAT CAPTAIN

Captain O'Reilly lit another cigarette as he walked onto the boat deck. His first mate had control of the wheel, which gave the Captain a moment to enjoy the nighttime mist from the river. City lights from the epicenter of downtown blurred in the thin layer of fog that always seemed to float along with the ship. The rhythmic bounce of the boat calmed O'Reilly, grounding him, the only time he felt somewhat at peace and in control.

Usually he took this chance to enjoy the quiet sounds of the distant city, but not tonight. Adams High School was hosting its prom dance on the boat's wide-open party deck. The sounds of seniors shouting, hip-hop bass reverberating, and general chaos echoed from the deck atop the ship. The sounds of genuine, carefree fun paired with the anxiety of *what's next.*

The Captain never quite had that experience of *what's next,* the anxiety that came when the unknown future met the expectations of the present. The Captain always knew. His father was a Captain, and his grandfather was a Captain. Fishing vessels that docked in Astoria. Some days they'd fish for massive ocean fish. Other times, especially during the salmon runs, they'd fish in the Columbia River. It was a hard life. Salt water blasted with the wind and the rain. Faces and hands weathered. Joints and bones rusted. Tough days meant long nights at the tavern to warm up, smoking all day and night to warm the lungs.

O'Reilly always knew he was going to be a Captain, but he knew he needed to leave Astoria and find a bigger pond. Feeling the vibration of the speakers on his own ship, he knew he'd made it there, but the gruffness of Astoria stayed with him, fused to his core.

Hosting prom on his prized vessel was a spectacle. Teenagers dressed in their finest rented tuxedos and ball gowns, top hats, stilettos, and gold chains, up-dos, up-downs, and buzz cuts. O'Reilly despised the show. He took pride in in ship, but he recoiled each time he was charged with chauffeuring these kids through the city down the Willamette River; prom nights always came with loud antics, rude youngsters, and pretentious knuckleheads who hadn't had a real day of struggle in their coddled little lives.

O'Reilly exhaled; a puff of smoke hovered above his head before being swept away by the Portland mist.

A fast-paced clanking sound jolted him from his time of meditation. He whipped around to see a student dashing down the metal staircase, a route reserved specifically for crew members. *Must have evaded the chaperones*, O'Reilly thought. The student jumped the last step and planted his feet firmly on the ground, moving briskly through the balcony corridor toward the deck, unaware that the Captain could see him. O'Reilly watched, shadowed from the moonlight. The kid wore an expression of desperation along with his red, fitted tuxedo and fedora.

"Hey there," O'Reilly shouted gruffly.

The student froze midstep, startled by the voice from the shadows. His dark skin illuminated in the moonlight.

"You're not supposed to be down here," the Captain continued. "Get back upstairs to the dance floor. It's not safe for you kids down here."

The kid took an aggressive step toward the Captain, who leaned against the cold metal post. A rivet dug into his shoulder.

"You can't tell me what to do, old man," the kid shouted. "Who you think you are?"

The Captain felt his right hand flex, an instinct born from his own days as a student, his own survival mechanism. He took another puff of his cigarette to redirect himself, and then he flicked the cigarette over the balcony. The red ember faded into the fog before it sunk into the river.

"Well, son," O'Reilly said, "I happen to be the Captain of this ship that you have the pleasure of cruising on this evening."

The kid relaxed his tension slightly.

"You're the Captain of this old thing?" the student asked.

"You bet I am," the Captain said, smiling through his

bristled gray beard.

Nervously adjusting his fedora, the kid slunk his shoulder. The confidence that only comes with a certain amount of adrenaline was gone. He seemed to shrink into his tuxedo.

"What are you doing down here, kid?" the Captain asked.

"Why do you care?" the kid fired back, still grasping to his defensive projection.

The Captain thought seriously about this question. *Why do I care? He's just some punk kid.*

"Well, for starters, you're down here in my territory, where my crew is working, on *my* ship," the Captain said. "What brought you down here?"

The kid jammed his hands in his pockets. He looked at his shoes, which shined in the glint of the moonlight. The mist from the river gave them an added layer of shine. He moved them nervously back and forth to the faint hip-hop bass that continued to echo from the dance floor above.

"Some guy kissed my girl," he said.

The Captain raised an eyebrow. *That's a fair reason to lay into someone*, he thought. The kid saw the Captain's eyebrow, and continued.

"I mean, my date and I aren't officially dating or anything, but I like her. And the guy knew that I liked her. And, I mean, he went and kissed her anyway."

He paused and gnawed on the inside of his cheek.

"I want to knock him out," the kid said. "Throw his ass off this boat."

The Captain smiled. He vaguely recalled a similar incident from his own high school prom. A long time ago. Back in

Astoria. His high school was much smaller than this one. Only about 100 students.

The dance was held at a dance hall on a pier that overlooked the end of the Columbia River, where the river met the Pacific Ocean. The meeting was violent. Turbulent. Warm water met cold water; freshwater met salt. Opposing currents crashed, each with the will to win.

Eileen, his prom date, had danced with another boy, an older boy who graduated the year before, but still lived and worked at the cannery nearby. O'Reilly was furious, his rage fueled by adolescence and whiskey.

He caught the boy outside on the dock, nearly tripping on the warped wooden boards. The boy was talking with Eileen. He offered her his coat. O'Reilly saw her take the coat, and he snapped. He tackled the boy onto the dock, punched him in the nose, slugged him in the ribs, drove his elbow into his abdomen.

When Eileen finally pulled O'Reilly off the boy, he saw the wreckage. The boy slithered in pain, blood dripping from his nose, bruising already beginning to form around his left eye. Ashamed and panicked, O'Reilly ran. And kept running. He ran down the dock until it connected with the street, and then he continued up the hill. He ran until his lungs burned. And then he sat.

O'Reilly looked through the darkness and saw a distant lighthouse casting its beam into the abyss of the sea. He looked at his hands; blood trickled down his knuckles from where he punched the boy. A splinter stuck into the space between his knuckles; he missed a punch and hit the dock.

He sat on that isolated hill all night until the sun began to rise above the hills. The whiskey had worn off. His head throbbed slightly. As he made his way down the hill, he walked to the boy's house. His hand throbbed as he knocked on the door. The boy answered, eyes almost swollen shut.

The act of apologizing, reducing oneself to humility, was nearly excruciating, but O'Reilly did it. At the end of the apology, they shook hands as equals, each wincing with pain, but recognizing the pain in the other.

Now, as O'Reilly stood on his own ship, he recognized the pain in the young student. The feeling of helplessness, agony, and defeat.

"So, you want to slug this kid, huh?" the Captain asked.

"He deserves it for kissing my date," the kid said.

"He probably does," the Captain said. "You want my advice?"

The student adjusted his fedora again.

"I guess."

"Alright," the Captain said. "Don't do it. There are plenty of other girls out there. In another month, you'll be done with high school. I know it seems like your whole world right now, but I promise you, kid, there's a whole big world out there full of other dates, other girls, and other ships."

The kid frowned a little, but looked up at the Captain.

"I know, I know," the kid said. "I just want him to hurt, just like I'm hurting."

The Captain smiled.

"I'll tell you what we're going to do, son," the Captain said. "Today, you get to be the bigger man. You want to show your date how much of a man you are? How tough you are? Show her you can do the toughest thing in the world."

The kid looked quizzically at the Captain.

"What's that?" he asked.

"Forgive."

THE AFFILIATE

He didn't want to do it, but he had to. It was the rules. If he didn't do it, they'd come after him. If he didn't do it, he couldn't fit in. He wouldn't have protection. And he needed protection. Badly.

The full moon moved behind the clouds, hiding its light from the street. Soft rain fell from the sky, more of a mist than a rain. He moved through the mist like a boat without a guiding light.

Cracked sidewalks were coated with a thin layer of moisture, like most sidewalks in North Portland. Over time, moss had filled the cracks, soaking up the city's moisture and making a home in the unformidable concrete, safe from the predators that target the bigger plants. Here, the moss just had to worry about being stepped on. Regularly.

Curtis flipped his hood over his head, shoved his hands in his pockets, and walked along the sidewalk, purposefully

179

avoiding the cracks. This was partly superstitious; he remembered an old rhyme he and his friends used to say about stepping on the cracks breaking momma's back. Curtis loved his mother, so he always avoided stepping on the disheveled pieces of sidewalk. He also recognized that puddles formed in the overlooked sections of the concrete and he didn't want to mess up his shoes if he didn't have to.

His sweatshirt hood slowly became damp, but his denim jacket kept the rain off his core. Luckily, his hands stayed dry in his jacket pockets. His left hand crunched up into a fist. His right hand gripped the gun, just to make sure it was still there.

Curtis had only ever held a gun once before, not with intent of using it, but just because it was there. He remembered it vividly, even though it was almost ten years ago.

After walking home from second grade, he went into his living room to turn on the television and watch cartoons like he did every day after school. His parents usually weren't home until dinnertime, so he could watch at least an hour of cartoons and they would never know. He was thirsty, so he went into the kitchen to grab a glass of water. All the cups on his level were gone; they must have been in the dishwasher. Curtis pushed a chair up to the counter, climbed onto the countertop, and reached into the top shelf to grab a coffee mug. He couldn't see that high up, but he could feel around. He felt something cold, something powerful. He knew it wasn't a cup.

He pulled the gun down from the top shelf, examining its

grooves, its craftsmanship, its power. It was just like he had seen in the movies. He aimed it at the cereal box character on the kitchen table and pretended to pull the trigger.

"Bang, bang, bang," he shouted through the empty house.

He stood there, aiming, one eye closed. He felt like a cowboy, or like a gangster. Like the guys he saw walking down his street after dark. Like the guys who showed up sometimes to talk to his dad, the guys who always dressed in blue, the guys who called him "Little Man" and "Young Brotha".

He went back into the living room and found one of his action figures. He aimed the gun, closed one eye, and pretended to shoot.

"Bang, bang, bang," he shouted again.

The front door opened.

Curtis froze.

His father stood in the doorway, looking at Curtis, gun pointing at his action figures, eyes bugged out.

"Son," his father said, "I need you to stay where you are and let me take that from you."

Curtis, too scared to move, did exactly as his father asked. His father put the gun on the counter and gave Curtis a hug, a genuine, protective, father-like hug.

That was one of the last times Curtis saw his dad, who was almost halfway through his sentence at a prison in Central Oregon. Armed robbery. With the guys in blue.

Without his father as a protector, Curtis was vulnerable to getting beat up by older kids who wore red, especially on the walk home from school. As he moved into middle school, he was vulnerable to getting stopped by the cops just for carrying a backpack. He also felt vulnerable to the growing number of self-righteous white people who seemed to be moving in around his neighborhood.

Without his father as a protector, the guys in blue had filled the role. They hung around Curtis's house, on his porch, at the dinner table. They walked him to and from school sometimes. They made sure no one messed with him. They made sure his mother had enough money for groceries. But Curtis was grown now, a tall, lanky 16-year-old man. He could take care of himself and his mother. But it came with a price.

In order to repay the guys in blue for their services, Curtis now had to become one of them. Well, he didn't *have* to. But there was serious pressure. And maybe he even *wanted* to become one of them. He wanted to give back to his community. He wanted that form of protection, and he wanted to protect.

He met with the leaders of the guys in blue a few times. They said he was in, under one condition. He had to do this one *little* thing. A guy in red from a few blocks over had messed with their revenue stream, so it was Curtis's job to take care of the situation. He handed Curtis a gun. Serial numbers scratched off. Toss it in the river when it's done.

He walked with his head up, careful not to step on the cracks in the sidewalk. He walked slowly, methodically, thinking about what he had to do. He couldn't do it. There was no way he could do it. This would ruin him. He'd freak out, he'd get scared, he'd try and miss. Something was going to go wrong.

Or worse. He *would* do it.

He had to do it. He couldn't back out now.

He stopped in the middle of the sidewalk. The smell of a cigar cut through the crisp Portland mist. Curtis looked straight up at the streetlight; rain coated his face. He paced a few steps forward, a few steps back, hands fishing around in his jacket pocket, resenting the weight of the gun.

"Hey, young brotha," an old man shouted from the porch. "What you doin' out here this late at night. Shouldn't you be doin' your homework?"

Curtis jumped. His sneakers lifted an inch or two off the concrete. He whipped his head around to see a well-lit porch.

"Uh, just walkin'," Curtis stammered. "I got somewhere to be."

The old man smiled.

"Come here, son," the old man said. "Sit with me for a while. I don't have many people to talk to these days."

Curtis hesitated. He had to keep moving, had to get the job done. But as he continued to convince himself to keep moving, he felt his legs carry him toward the house.

The old house was a North Portland original. White people would love to get their hands on this house and "fix it up." The wide porch was well-hidden with rose bushes. If it wasn't for the porchlight, Curtis never would have known it existed.

Leaning back in his wooden rocking chair, the old man puffed on his cigar. He tipped up the brim of his paperboy hat, a hat that had been worn from years of experience. His clean-shaven face revealed deep wrinkles, but not wrinkles that society would deem "ugly". They gave him an aura of wisdom, wrinkles that had formed around the eyes from laughter, and on the forehead from thinking.

The old man motioned for Curtis to take a seat in the other rocking chair. He held up an unlit cigar.

"Want a smoke, son?" he asked.

"No thanks," Curtis said, sitting heavily in the chair.

The old man smiled.

"What are you doin' out at this time of night, Curtis?" the old man asked.

"Just walkin'," he said.

Curtis paused and looked at the old man.

"Hey, hold up. How'd you know my name was Curtis?"

The old man smiled, the wrinkles on his forehead furrowed wisely.

"I've been in this neighborhood a long time, son," the old man said. "I even knew your daddy when *he* was a kid, runnin' around these streets without a care in the world."

Curtis leaned forward.

"You knew my dad?"

"Sure did," the old man said.

He stuck out his hand to shake Curtis's. His hand shook slightly. So did Curtis's, but for a different reason.

"Raymond," the old man said.

"Nice to meet you, Raymond."

They both leaned back in their chairs. Raymond puffed his cigar, releasing a billow of smoke into the air.

"Like I said, son, I've been in this neighborhood a long time," Raymond said. "I've seen some things, I've done some things, I've learned some things."

Curtis raised an eyebrow at the cryptic statement.

"I remember a time, after the war, when our people moved here from all around the country to work. We all congregated up here in the North, by the river, by the shipyards, you see. That's why this is a black neighborhood. Anyway, we were doin' just fine up here until some white folks started hasslin' us, you know, like they do."

He smiled knowingly at Curtis, who returned the acknowledgement.

"Now, of course we knew the cops weren't going to protect us," Raymond continued. "Shoot, they were harassin' us even more than regular white folks. We had to form our own groups to protect *ourselves*. Self-reliance, like Ralph Emerson talked about. That white boy was onto somethin'."

He smiled at the thought of it.

"Our form of self-protection started out positive. We had guns, of course, but we couldn't let the government or the cops know about them because they don't want *us* to be armed. Hell, they scared of us. So, we kept everything quiet."

Curtis leaned in, rocking on his toes with the rhythm of the story.

"We were making decent money in the shipyards, but after they busted up our union, they started paying us like garbage. Neo-slavery. They started raising rent *while* cutting our pay, forcing us to work longer, harder hours, away from our families. So, our people had to find *other* ways to make money, whether it was inside or outside the system."

The weight of the gun pulled Curtis forward.

"Unfortunately, the development of gang culture in our

neighborhood was bound to happen," Raymond said. "It was our way of protecting ourselves, providing for our own. It started out as a necessity. It turned into a trap, damn near impossible for a youngin' like you to avoid."

Raymond motioned his head toward the unlit cigar that rested by a half-full glass of apple juice on the small table. Curtis reached for it. Raymond snagged it quickly, cut it, and then passed it to Curtis. He lit it clumsily, coughing as he puffed. Raymond smirked, remembering his early days smoking cigars after work at the shipyards.

"When I ran the boys in blue," Raymond continued, "we didn't have that violence in us. Sure, we were rebellious and rowdy and talked a lot of smack to white folks and cops, but we didn't have no violent intentions. Nowadays, y'all be runnin' around waving guns and talkin' about revenge and nonsense. We used our weapons for protection from the outside world, not against each other. When you step back and think, who do these gangs seek out for revenge? Not the system that keeps us oppressed, that's for damn sure."

Curtis nodded in agreement. He had never thought about the system like that before. A system he was powerless to fight against, to stand up against. A system he couldn't escape. Or could he?

"We ought to be building our own community up with these groups, not battling against each other for so-called *turf*," Raymond said. "The boys in blue started gettin' that revenge mentality, and that's when I got out. I realized there was something more I could do than run around with that worldview."

"You got out?" Curtis asked. "Like, you were runnin' with them and then just…got out?"

Raymond smiled. Smoke slowly rolled through his teeth and billowed around his hat.

"Sure did," he said. When you're in the thick of it, it seems like you don't have any other option. And once you reach a certain point of what they call *loyalty*, it gets tougher and tougher to walk away. But we human. We always have a choice to control our own lives and make things better for ourselves and the world around us in our own way."

Both rocking chairs moved in slow rhythm. Curtis nodded with every forward motion.

Then, Raymond stopped rocking. He looked at Curtis with conviction, with a calm sense of wisdom and purpose.

"Now, give me that tool in your pocket," Raymond said. "I'll take care of it. As long as you promise to find another path, one without so many cracks and slick spots.

Curtis handed his gun to the old man, who placed it on the table. He removed his hat and set it on top of the gun.

"You best be gettin' home now," Raymond said. "And tomorrow, know that you've made a choice for *you*. It won't be easy. I never said it would be, but you'll find your purpose. And I can tell you, this thing under my hat, this ain't it."

Curtis smiled. He stood and nodded to Raymond; the cigar smoldered in his hand.

"Thank you for your time, sir," Curtis said. "I appreciate you."

He jogged down the stairs and strolled across the grass and onto the sidewalk. Curtis noticed a small flower sprouting from a crack in the concrete; he stepped around it carefully. Standing under the streetlight, he looked back at Raymond. Cigar smoke swirled around his head, outlined by the porch light.

"Somethin' tells me I'll be seeing you around," Raymond shouted.

"You will, sir."

THE HIPPIE

A cyclist charged toward Gregory, who danced unaware that impending doom moving at him with precision and speed. On the paved pathway that lined the river, Gregory embraced the beauty of the day, dancing to invite positivity into his life, expelling the bad auras and vibes that might be lurking inside him.

"Move over, you weirdo!" the cyclist shouted as he sped by, almost clipping Gregory, who bobbed up and down, slightly off-beat.

The weekend's jazz festival kicked off the day before, and they had started up again early. The quiet city was still waking up. Saxophone notes and rhythmic drums floated through the air along the river. Skidmore Fountain spouted gloriously; dew glistened in the morning sunlight, a rarity in the springtime.

Gregory saw other people dancing, too. Some early risers

strolled along the pathway with their morning coffees, a habit that he viewed as particularly unclean. Caffeine interfered with the natural endorphins of the body. So did alcohol. Gregory was aware of these facts, which was why he chose to abstain from anything that would cloud his mind, anything that would dampen his physical awareness of the world around him. He ate only organic vegetables, choosing to ignore meat. He only partook in substances that would *expand* the mind.

And that's what this morning was all about: expanding his mind.

His long hair flowed as he moved his way down the path. His backpack inhibited his hair's motion, but Gregory wasn't concerned about that. He noticed how the music notes flowed in the same direction as the river, but the river moved against the wind he could see. The golden sunshine warmed him; he felt the color of gold absorb into his pores.

Bobbing to the beat of nature rather than the drums, he paused, noticing the message displayed on a hand-drawn sign. The man holding it seemed happy, content to sit cross-legged in the patchy grass along the path. The sign read: *Keep Portland Weird.*

"Right on, man," Gregory said to the man with the sign.

The man nodded back enthusiastically.

The affirmation struck Gregory as significant. Profound, even. Gregory bounded over to the railing and focused on the river. A boat floated up the water. As it approached the Hawthorne Bridge, the bridge lifted, allowing the boat to pass underneath it before lowering again.

It's alright if people perceive me as weird, Gregory thought. *Sometimes, I just need permission to keep on going, just like that little boat. Like, who cares what these people around me think. If I need to dance to get my body in tune with my surroundings, who cares about these people and what they think. I'm here for me and the world, not for the judgement of these people. I can be what they might see as weird. I think they're weird for not dancing and smiling.*

He dug his bare toe into a groove in the cement.

Like, my parents just don't get it, he continued. *If they knew how connected the mind and the body were, they would understand my choice. I mean, so what if they gave me some expensive private school education? It didn't teach me anything useful. It just put me in the same room with a bunch of other snobs who didn't really care about the world. Who cares if I didn't graduate from college? It's not my fault that the way I thought was different than what those so-called professors wanted me to think. Just because I didn't buy into the establishment doesn't mean I'm weird.*

If my parents knew how much power the interconnected mind-body has on the world around them, they would be right here with me. Not in their expensive house in the hills, overlooking these people that they just view as peasants.

It's like we're back in the Medieval Era, but no one even notices. People just do what they're parents tell them. If I was born poor, I would be working and working and working and that would be my life. Just working. But all these rich people don't even know what to do either, so they just work and work and don't even stop to think, or to appreciate the world around them. And people treat each other so badly. I mean, look at all these homeless people that don't have food, and all these people with their ten-dollar coffees just walk by them like they don't even exist. It's barbaric, man.

Gregory saw a jogger approaching; he wore expensive athletic gear. Gregory glared at him, forcing his mental energy to influence the jogger's mind and awareness that he was part of the problem.

It's wild how everything in the body is so connected, Gregory thought. *If I tell myself something in my mind, I'll start to believe it. If I start to believe, I'll start to do it. And if I channel that same energy outward and project it into the world, I can literally change the world, one person at a time.*

Gregory continued his dance-walk down the path toward the jazz festival. He had no intention of paying to get in; rather, he was pulled there by the music.

My parents think I'm crazy, Gregory thought. *They disagree with my lifestyle choice, my choice to live in poverty and get in tune with the world. But they're the ones that are crazy. Just working. Me, though. I'm just living my life on my own terms. Not theirs. Not society's. My own terms. They probably think it makes them look bad in front of their friends, whose kids are all doctors and lawyers and whatever else society tells them is successful. But are they happy? Not a chance, man. I'm happy. Isn't that all a parent should want for their kids?*

The security guard at the north entrance of the jazz festival saw Gregory coming from under the bridge: long hair, tattered shirt, cut-off jeans, no shoes, and a grungy backpack. The smell of marijuana seemed to float along with him.

"Good morning, sir," the woman said.

Gregory smiled warmly, as he always did when he received a positive vibration from another encounter.

"Well, good morning, ma'am," Gregory said. "Are you enjoying the music this morning?"

His voice seemed to echo and float as he hung on to each vowel.

"I sure am," the woman said. "Do you have a ticket? Or would you like to purchase one from the counter over there?"

"Oh, I don't have a ticket," he said. "I just wanted to feel some music today."

"Alright," the security guard said. "You can go over here and purchase a day pass then."

"Why thank you," Gregory said, "but I won't be needing a ticket just to feel some music."

The security guard tapped a button on her radio that signaled the need for an extra guard.

"Actually, sir, you do need a ticket to enter through these gates," she said.

This is ridiculous, Gregory thought. *Why can't I just walk in? I mean, I was born just up the hill from here. If this lady only knew who my parents were. My parents' tax money practically pays for this entire park anyway. She thinks that she can just tell me "no" and think that I'm just going to take that answer as acceptable? I just want to vibe, man. Let me through. I'm not going to pay for the gift of music and have this money just line the pockets of...*

The smell of a food truck from inside the festival gates wafted to Gregory's nose. Grilled peppers, onions, and teriyaki sauce.

The impulse to eat overcame his impulse to fight the power of authority with the mentality of a bourgeoisie man who strived to think like a member of the proletariat.

Gregory stomped over to the ticket counter; each stomp in the grass expelled just a little more frustration. Reluctantly, he paid for a day pass with cash from his back pocket, cash that he received from his parents each month, cash that he had never been without.

As Gregory passed through the gate, he heard jazz notes waft through the air, accompanied by the scent of street tacos. He followed his nose to the food truck.

THE PRIEST

Father Gabriel approached the wooden lectern, holding his church's ornate Bible above his head, half-singing a phrase he had repeated thousands of times. His muscles didn't fire like they used to, and his joints were becoming more arthritic by the day, but he still felt a rush every time he approached the lectern to speak. It was the highlight of his week.

After reading a story from the *Book of Luke*, he closed his Bible and stepped down from the lectern. He moved down from the altar and into the aisle where he could be closer to his parishioners. He didn't like to deliver a homily from the lectern itself; it made him feel too pompous, too authoritative. He rather enjoyed intermingling with his parishioners while he preached; it felt more authentic.

Father Gabriel wasn't from the upper class, anyway. He was born and raised in a family who lived paycheck to paycheck. Serving parishioners who came from impoverished situations and blue-collar working backgrounds made him feel rather at home.

As he stood in front of the crowd, he began to speak about humility, the major theme of his homily. Father Gabriel used Pope Francis as an example of someone who had risen to one of the highest offices in the world, yet he decided to reduce the scope of elegance and show that the office had exhibited for nearly 2,000 years. Where Popes used to wear gaudy robes, golden shoes, and luxurious jewelry, Pope Francis decided to cut down on those displays of wealth, opting for more humble clothing and less audacious festivities.

Father Gabriel went on to say that acts of humility like that inspired him to do the same. As a young priest, Gabriel had opted to follow Pope Francis's example and wear simple robes, focusing his efforts more on doing good works in the community than putting on a show for his parishioners.

He said he always tried to remain humble and learn from those who led by an example of humility, though he acknowledged that it was easier said than done.

After the rest of the mass had finished, Father Gabriel approached the lectern again, this time for closing remarks about after-church activities.

"*Hoy, tenemos café en nuestra cocina,*" Father Gabriel said. "*Espero verte allí.*"

He looked around the audience to see how many non-verbal signals he could read to indicate whether or not he would have a high rate of attendance at this week's after-church coffee session. He hoped no one would show up so he could return to his room and relax. It had been a difficult week. Extra masses for special members of the community. Additional community service projects to help students on summer vacation stay out of trouble. An entire day spent at the seminary helping soon-to-be priests finish their training. He was exhausted, pushed to the physical limit. He needed sleep, and he was getting tired of talking to people today. He stated a few more closing remarks, the formal exit phrase and finished it off with his signature *Gracias a Dios*.

The crowd filtered out of the church, recongregating on the cement platform. The parishioners who sat in the front row exited last, pushing the overflow crowd members into the parking lot. Humidity filled the air as it did every time the sun warmed the rainy pavement. The rain had washed away the dust that sometimes gathered on the sidewalks during the summertime.

Father Gabriel moved gracefully through the crowd; his simple robes allowed him to move without much constriction. A familiar, well-dressed man approached Father Gabriel and shook his hand. His dark suit and green tie projected an image of power, of status, of a desire to be seen. His jet-black hair contrasted severely with Father Gabriel's bald head.

"Mr. Bartolo, how are you this morning?" Father Gabriel asked.

"I'm doing well, *Padre*," he said. "I quite enjoyed your homily about humility and learning from the experiences of others."

Father Gabriel forced sincerity into his smile.

"Well thank you," Father Gabriel said. "I always hope that our community gets at least something out of my message."

A layer of tobacco film coated Mr. Bartolo's teeth, which began to pop out underneath his thin mustache.

"Speaking of humility, I was thinking about next month's charity banquet," Mr. Bartolo said. "I wanted to make a generous donation to the church because, as you might have heard, my business is doing extremely well this year."

Father Gabriel nodded impartially.

"I was wondering, though, *Padre*," Mr. Bartolo continued, "since the donation will be large, I want my name to be placed prominently inside the church entryway. If not, that's fine. We're considering a few other organizations to donate our money, so if the Church doesn't cooperate."

Father Gabriel seemed to look through Mr. Bartolo, noticing a mother and her three small children standing in the crowd. The mother looked sad. No, not sad. Exhausted.

Though she wore a smile, her eyes showed how tired she was. How much she had sacrificed to give these three children an opportunity.

"Thank you for your consideration, Mr. Bartolo," Father Gabriel said. "We'll talk about this soon."

Father Gabriel patted Mr. Bartolo on the shoulder assertively, as a subtle condemnation.

Walking toward the mother and her children, Father Gabriel wondered where they had come from. He knew they hadn't been to church before. Were they trying out a new neighborhood church? Or maybe they had just moved to Portland from another part of the state. Or, perhaps, another country, like he himself had.

Seven years ago, Father Gabriel moved to Portland from Lima, Peru. He spoke little English, just enough to get by. He was placed in a church in the West Hills. That placement was short-lived; the white, English-speaking parishioners of Portland's upper crest didn't feel like they were being served properly by a foreigner. So, the diocese placed Father Gabriel in Northeast Portland, where there were many more Spanish speakers. He was able to use his language and culture to positively influence that neighborhood, and he began to feel more connected almost immediately.

But the move from Peru to the United States exhausted Gabriel. He knew he had a message to send, but it was difficult to convey the message properly to a culture that wasn't used to hearing this type of message. A message of humility. A message of poverty overcoming the riches of American life, that it was easier for a camel to pass through the Eye of the Needle than for a rich man to make it into Heaven. That the poor shall inherit the Kingdom of Heaven.

People in the West Hills were not ready to receive this message. People in his new neighborhood, though, they just might be. Not people like Mr. Bartolo. But people like this mother.

"*Hola,*" Father Gabriel said with a soft-yet-commanding tone. "*Bienvenidos a nuestra iglesia.*"

The woman smiled meekly.

"Thank you," she said. "It's our first time here."

"I thought it might be," Father Gabriel said. "We're glad to have you. What's your name?"

"Teresa," she said. "And these are my kids: Chris, Madeline, and Antonio."

Father Gabriel smiled sweetly.

"Where are you coming to us from?" Father Gabriel asked. "Another church nearby?"

The woman looked back over her shoulder. Her eyebrows narrowed; her lips seemed to shrink. Her vocal volume became a whisper.

"I've come from Mexico," she said. "Not my kids. They were born here, but I came from Mexico."

The kids began to squirm with pent-up energy from sitting in an hour-long church service. Chris flicked Antonio's ear; Antonio punched him in the arm. Madeline stuck her hands out to control their unruly behavior.

Father Gabriel saw the pain that hid behind her eyes. Her eyes told him about her struggles to remain safe after her husband was arrested for stealing food because their city faced a drought, a crop shortage. Her eyes told him about the fear of incoming triplets without a father and without an income. Her eyes told him about the journey from central Mexico to the border, about the fear that she would be caught by the U.S. border patrol, or worse. Her eyes told him about raising triplets on her own in a foreign country, a country that told her to leave each and every day. Her eyes told her about the exhaustion of working two full-time jobs, earning minimum wage, just to keep food on the table for her three children, lucky if there was any left for her most days.

"*No pasa nada,*" Father Gabriel said. "*No soy de aquí tampoco. Soy de Peru.* I'm glad you're here."

Teresa smiled. Her eyes told Father Gabriel that she felt acknowledged, seen, understood. Her eyes told him that a little moment like this, of recognition, of respect, made her day, her week.

Immediately, Father Gabriel felt rejuvenated. This was serving the community. This was spreading his message, the message of the Lord, the message of humility, and the simple complexity of a human connection.

THE HOMELESS MAN

Eddy lifted his camouflage cap and wiped his brow with his sleeve. Grime covered his white, weathered hands. The overcast sky was unusually hot. Or maybe it was the long-sleeved shirt and overcoat that he wore. He couldn't take them off, though. Someone would definitely steal them. And besides, they were all he had. That and a water bottle that a priest had given.

Earlier in the day, he had managed to scrounge up some cardboard, which he sawed into two pieces using his knife, a weapon he had carried with him everywhere since the mid 70s. Sweat beaded underneath his gray, scraggly beard as he wrote on the cardboard sign with a black marker he found by the curb.

Vietnam War vet. Need cash for food. Anything will help. God bless.

He knew this was a familiar message to people, and it

often worked in securing enough money to make it through the day, sometimes even through the week if he could snag the right corner. Like most businesses, this one was all about location.

He walked toward the Broadway Bridge; its red cage encased cars as they zoomed across the Willamette River as evening rush hour began. Some probably went to their high paying jobs. Others came home from their high paying jobs. A nice dinner and trash television awaited them. What a boring existence. Such predictability.

Eddy scanned the open street corners by the bridge. His competition was fierce, and he didn't want to get mixed up in a territorial dispute again. Certain corners around town were known for a high panhandling payout, but these corners were protected ferociously. Eddy had been in the panhandling game for a few decades now, and knew the unwritten rules, the code he must follow to protect his own supply while still capitalizing on his profit.

He knew that the highest profit came from the stop lights with the most traffic. Loads of cars would have to stop at the light moving out of downtown, the light just before the bridge. With only so many bridges in and out of the city, staking a claim along a bridge stop light was prime real estate. These traffic routes didn't belong to non-stop freeway traffic; they belonged to slow traffic with frequent stops. And the frequent stops meant he could look drivers in the eye, guilt trip them with his sign, and receive their charity.

Unfortunately, most members of the homeless community in Portland knew these tactics too. The bigger people, the ones with more resources, and the ones with backup controlled most of the profitable corners: the Hawthorne Bridge, Steel Bridge, Convention Center, and Pioneer Courthouse Square. The Broadway Bridge tended to be too far north, an afterthought. As a result, its corners were usually open.

Eddy laid claim to a corner and posted up against the stop light's beam. He set his pack down and stood with his sign facing oncoming traffic.

A red sports car sped toward the light, which turned yellow, and then quickly to red. The driver slammed on his breaks and threw his hands up to visibly show his disgust at the red light that had ruined his speed.

The frustrated driver looked angrily at Eddy. He rolled his window down and leaned his head out the window.

"You lazy bum!" the man shouted. "Why don't you get a real job?"

Anger snarled from the driver's seat. Eddy was accustomed to this type of beratement, so he simply held up two fingers to indicate peace.

The light turned green and the car sped off. Eddy saw a white middle finger protrude from the sports car's window, its paleness beaming as it moved across the bridge. Another line of cars sped through the short green light before piling up as the light turned red. At the front of the line, a white SUV waited patiently. A woman in her mid-40s rolled down her window and smiled at Eddy.

"I don't have any cash on me," the woman said. "But I do have a peanut butter and jelly sandwich. Would that help?"

"Thank you, ma'am," Eddy said graciously. "I would love that."

She reached over into the passenger seat, grabbed the sandwich, and held it out the window. Eddy jogged to the window and slowly took the sandwich, returning the kind gesture with a nod.

The light turned green and the car sped off. This time, a compassionate wave from the white SUV sealed the act of kindness with yet another one.

While he waited for the next red light, Eddy removed the sandwich from the plastic bag and took a bite. The perfect ratio of peanut butter to jelly. Not that it mattered. Any ratio would have sufficed. Eddy would have been fine with two pieces of bread. Aside from the half-eaten granola bar he found that morning, Eddy hadn't eaten in over 24 hours.

Eddy finished his sandwich just before the next red light. A black truck pulled up to the stop light, its engine revving to showcase its power. The tinted window rolled down and a large, white man leaned out of the window. His hat featured an American flag with a victorious looking eagle.

"Hey, man," the guy said. "You ain't even old enough to have fought in Vietnam. You're lying."

Eddy simply smiled, knowing this man knew nothing of his experience.

"How dare you use the sacrifices of those boys in Nam to get some free drug money," the man shouted. "You're a real piece of work, you know that?"

The man glared at Eddy with sincerity. True hate. The light turned green. Black smoke billowed from the truck's exhaust pipe as it sped across the bridge.

This left Eddy thinking about the smoky fields in Vietnam. The crops he had helped to burn to reduce the food supply of the Viet Cong. The men he had seen burned by napalm and obliterated by Agent Orange. The nights spent in rainy jungles, falling asleep to the sounds of mosquitos and gunfire.

He recalled the time when he was walking through a village on a mission to track down some Viet Cong spies that lived near a U.S. army base. As they walked through the village, he saw small children hiding in their wooden houses. Mothers clung to their children; true fear gripped them. One of his commanders grabbed a woman by the throat and shouted at her, demanding she tell him where the rebels were hiding. The woman didn't speak English. She shook her head in fear. The commander threw her down and shot her, right there on the dirt road. He ordered the rest of his company to shoot, and they followed orders. Eddy too. Dozens of innocent women and children sprawled dead in the street.

As he was firing, Eddy knew it wasn't right, but he had been trained to do whatever his commanding officers told him to do. He hated the war after that. He thought he was helping his country by fighting off Communism. But that's not what he was doing in Vietnam. He was killing mothers and children. He saw faces blown off by Vietnamese soldiers who just wanted to take control of their own country by these invading Americans. And he was part of it.

As more and more soldiers were asked to commit atrocities like these, Eddy and his fellow soldiers began to vehemently disagree with the war they had been drafted into involuntarily. This war was not just, and word was getting around through different military camps that it was only going to get worse. As more soldiers flew into Vietnam from the States, Eddy knew that the war was ramping up. There would be no winner. Vietnam was a pawn in the U.S. government's game to rule the world.

Eddy and his friends staged small acts of disobedience. They smoked, drank, and showed up late to check-ins. They fraternized with the "enemy". They gambled. They slept in. They slacked off during drills and exercises. Anything they could do to slow the progress of this dumb war they were forced into.

But that still didn't cleanse Eddy's conscience, or his memory. When he returned home after two years in Vietnam, he wasn't the same person at all. He had nightly flashbacks. The Fourth of July terrified him; fireworks sent him into fits of fear, hiding in closets and rolling on the floor.

He always envisioned returning home like a hero, like those soldiers in World War II. But they were fighting the Nazis. He was murdering families. And the American public knew that. He was hated. Wearing his uniform in public brought ridicule and disdain, and for good reason. Eddy couldn't live with himself for what he had seen, for what he had *done*.

He tried to talk about it to clear his mind, but the doctors just called it "shell shock". They told him it would pass. It didn't. Taking a few swigs of whiskey before bed would at least dull the nightmares. Starting the day with a swig or two would dull the memories and the reactions to the sounds of helicopters and backfiring cars.

Next thing he knew, he was 32 years old with no job, an empty savings account, and no one to support him. His parents were gone. His sister wouldn't lend him any more money. Eddy was overdue on rent for too many months. So, he spent the night on a bus bench with nothing but a large overcoat to keep him warm and his military-issued knife for protection.

And it had remained that way ever since.

An hour went by on the same street corner by the Broadway Bridge. Most people who stopped at the light didn't even look at Eddy. Most people knew that if they looked at him, they would feel guilty and give him money, or they would have to acknowledge their own selfishness. So, most people chose to ignore him, to keep looking straight ahead as if he was invisible.

And that's how he felt most days. Invisible.

Sure, there were some kind folks who stopped and gave him a few quarters, maybe even a couple dollars, but even their interactions were out of their own guilt. They didn't care what happened to Eddy, not in the past, present, and certainly not the future. He was invisible. A part of the city that no one wanted to see.

Light rain drops began to fall. Eddy looked up and saw the overcast skies getting thicker. And night was approaching. It was time to move on. Eddy put his money in his pack, 17 dollars. He smiled, knowing he would be able to eat. He also knew he would be able to buy a pint of whiskey.

He tossed his pack over his shoulders and grabbed his

sign. Hopefully he could use the sign for the next few days before the rain tore it to shreds.

As he began to leave, he saw a young man walking in his direction. The man grasped the hood of his raincoat and threw it over his head, speeding his pace to get somewhere before the rain picked up too much. Based on his clothing style, glasses, and headphones, he was probably a student, which meant he was not an ideal candidate to ask for spare change. So, Eddy made the choice to simply ignore him and let him pass without a hassle. But, to his surprise, the student stopped directly in front of Eddy.

"Hey there, sir," the student said. "I saw your sign. Are you really a Vietnam veteran?"

Eddy hesitated; he wasn't used to people asking about his past, or talking to him at all, for that matter.

"Yes," Eddy said. "Yes I am."

The student looked down at his feet as he built up the courage to ask the next question.

"I'm a student at Portland College and I'm taking a history class about the Vietnam War," the student said. "I'd love to hear your story."

Eddy smiled and nodded.

"I'd love to share my story with you.

"You know," the student said, "twice a week, I serve meals at that soup kitchen down the way. What do you say we get out of this rain and get you a hot meal?"

"I usually go for whiskey to keep me warm, but soup would be just fine."

They both laughed. The student reached his hand out to

shake Eddy's. His dark skin contrasted with Eddy's white, weathered hand.

"I'm Kenny," the student said.

"Pleasure to meet you, Kenny. I'm Eddy."

They smiled and started walking through the rain.

"So, what's your story, Eddy?"

THE VOLUNTEER

Esperanza's eyes burned from the steam that exploded out of the massive steel pot. The soup boiled fiercely, spouting broth through the slim opening in the lid. Drops scalded her forearms as she moved the pot from the industrial kitchen burner to the serving station in the front room. Dropping the heavy pot into its holder gave way to relaxation of her back muscles, but the steam remained on her brow in the form of condensation. Or perspiration. She wasn't quite sure.

She wiped her brow with her apron and scanned the room. Nearly empty, but a few people trickled in and found seats to claim their spots for the night's dinner. Dinner started promptly at 5:00 p.m. every night, but somehow, a few people always seemed to sneak through the doors at 4:49 on the dot. An old Vietnam War veteran sat in the corner with an uncharacteristic smile. Esperanza grinned and went back into the kitchen to grab another pot of boiling soup.

Every Wednesday night, Esperanza volunteered at The Open Table. It was a refreshing break from the mundanity of the corporate world in which she spent a majority of her time. After her kids left home to go to college, she found herself with plenty of spare time. Too much of it, in fact. She dove into her job even more than she already was, and she did so just to fill time. But it lacked fulfillment.

So, she found a weekly activity that filled that void. Something to counteract her daily corporate shuffle. She showed up to the kitchen, helped other volunteers and full-time workers cook dinner. And then, the best part of her week: serving dinner to Portland's homeless population.

At least, it used to be the best part of her week.

After serving at The Open Table for a little over seven months, Esperanza found herself growing more cynical. She watched as hundreds of homeless people flooded into the room, scooped their soup, gnashed their bread, and guzzled their juice. Faces started to become familiar, until she realized that she was seeing the same people each week.

Then she started to question her own actions. Was she really *helping* these people, or simply enabling them to continue living a life of laziness, inebriation, and misery? She hadn't had this discussion with anyone, of course. Talk like that was extremely taboo in the homeless shelter soup kitchen world. But the idea continued to grab hold of her.

As she stood in the kitchen waiting for the cornbread to finish baking, she looked around at a few other volunteers and wondered if they ever had similar thoughts, similar doubts. She felt guilty for even thinking this way, but her rational mind couldn't help it. The concept made too much sense, and she hadn't seen any statistics or personal examples to lead her toward a more positive outlook.

The oven timer rang and Esperanza opened the oven. Removing the cornbread, she placed it on the counter and checked the old analog wall clock: 4:58.

"Hey, Miguel," Esperanza said, "when these cool a little bit, cut them up and put them on this serving tray and bring them out for me. I'm going to head out into the dining room and start serving."

Miguel nodded and smiled, but Esperanza was already on her way out of the kitchen. She stood by the large vat of soup, which had cooled off quite a bit. Looking toward the already-formed line, she waved at the first person to begin.

An older man walked slowly toward Esperanza. He reached for a plate; his hand shook methodically as it moved. *Drugs or old age*, Esperanza theorized.

He strolled over to Esperanza, and she scooped a ladle full of soup and poured it into his bowl. He looked at her with kind eyes and thanked her. She couldn't tell if his kind expression was genuine, or simply a mask to feign gratitude to snag a freebie.

"How's your day going, sir?" Esperanza asked.

"Oh, just fine, I suppose," the man said.

"Weather's gettin' colder and rainier," Esperanza said. "How you holdin' up?"

The man smiled.

"Well, I got myself a nice place to stay down the street,"

the man said. "Waterproof roof over my head at least."

He nodded toward her, a period to end his story. He walked away to the juice station, and a younger woman filled his place to receive her soup. This woman was a regular. She looked a little more haggard than she did last week. Probably a result of either too many drugs, or not enough.

"*Que pasa, Silvia?*" Esperanza asked the woman.

"*El mismo como siempre,*" Silvia said.

"*Tienes una idea para un trabajo?*"

Silvia laughed a little. Her eyes rolled up a little too far into her skull.

"*No necesito tener una trabajo si dasme sopa cada semana,*" Silvia said.

The woman moved to the juice station; Esperanza's heart sank. Silvia had confirmed her suspicions: these people weren't making any effort to find a job or get their lives on track, and being fed free soup wasn't helping the situation. The expression of disappointment was visible.

Another familiar regular, a middle-aged man with salt-and-pepper hair, approached the soup station. Esperanza dug her ladle into the stock pot, ready to fill his bowl, but he held his bowl back, not ready to receive help. He looked at Esperanza quizzically, reading her expression.

"Well, my dear," the man said, "I just wanted to thank you for helping us out. You have no idea how much this meal means to us."

"Aw, thanks Herman," Esperanza said flatly.

Herman nodded knowingly.

"You know, this is the only food I eat all day," he

continued. "I depend on this meal every single night. Without you all helping us out, I'd probably starve to death."

Esperanza smiled and shook off the compliment.

"I'm serious," Herman continued. "You know, it's impossible to get a job without a home address. And it's impossible to get a home address without money from a job. Without a job, I can't buy no food. It's an endless cycle, really. And without you, I wouldn't have any food to eat."

"It's our pleasure to serve you, sir," Esperanza said.

"Esperanza," he continued, "it's no secret I've got some mental issues. Hearin' voices sometimes. But I can't afford a doctor. I can't afford no pills. Shoot, I don't even have any family alive that'll take me in, or even keep an eye on me."

Esperanza's conscience began to fill with guilt.

"The only thing that makes me feel sane sometimes is the drugs," Herman said. "And I know they're no good for me, but I can't find another solution."

Esperanza looked down at the simmering soup. The steam rose toward the top of the pot, turning to liquid when it came into contact with the lid that half-covered it.

"I'm truly sorry, Herman," she said. "That must be a very difficult situation to deal with."

"Sure is," he said. "All of us in here have one situation or another keeping us down. Some of us are too prideful to admit it. Shoot, for some of us, even accepting a free meal is too much for our egos to handle."

Herman nodded toward Silvia, who sat alone on the far side of the room slurping her soup.

"Take Silvia, for example," he said. "She'd been kicked out

of more abusive foster homes than she can count. And she damn sure ain't admitting she needs help. But she does."

Esperanza smiled empathetically.

"She might not show her gratitude," Herman said, "but she *is* thankful for your help, Esperanza."

Herman held his bowl out in front of Esperanza's pot of soup. She filled it and watched the steam rise. Herman nodded, smiled, and made his way slowly to the juice station.

Next in line was a young mother that Esperanza had seen over the last few months. She recognized the woman's long, black hair and smooth brown skin that resembled her own. Esperanza also recognized her daughter, who always clung to her legs as they moved through the soup line.

"*Julietta, como estas?*" Esperanza asked.

"*Muy bien, Esperanza,*" Julietta said. "*Este sopa es la mejor parte de mi dia.*"

She looked down toward her daughter and smiled sadly. Esperanza poured a scoop of soup into her bowl, and then she reached across the table to grab another bowl for Julietta's daughter. Even though each visitor was only allowed one plate each, Esperanza always made an exception for Julietta; she hated to see this little girl go hungry.

"*Gracias, en serio,*" Julietta said. "It's people like you, Esperanza, that give people like us hope."

Esperanza felt her heart flutter. Her cheeks flushed at the compliment.

"You know, I'm trying to find a job," Julietta said. "I found a shelter to take me and my daughter in. It'll get us off the streets. It's a women's shelter."

Esperanza nodded approvingly and smiled.

"Good for you, Julietta."

"And another good part is that I can use the shelter as my home address," she continued. "Maybe I can finally find some temporary work, now that I'll have an address. I can work somewhere nearby. Maybe start to save some money to rent an apartment."

Esperanza filled Julietta's bowl with soup, and then filled the daughter's bowl.

"I don' t think we would have made it to this point without this place, without people like you," Julietta said. "We don't want to be homeless, but it's a hard situation to escape. Without this food, my daughter and I probably would have died."

She looked at Esperanza with grave sincerity. Picking up her soup bowl, Julietta began to walk away, but turned and stood firmly in place in front of the pot.

"Thank you for being such a light, Esperanza."

THE INTELLECTUAL

The barista walked across the coffee shop carrying four coffees on a tray. He weaved between tables with agility. The rough floorboards were original. They added ambiance to the trendy coffee shop, just like the exposed brick and the wide-open windows that provided a view of a busy pedestrian side street. But the barista always worried about tripping, especially when he approached the window. After nearly 100 years of Pacific Northwest rain, the original floorboards near the front of the open room had warped severely.

He saw a problematic floorboard sticking up above the rest. He knew it was there. He tripped on it every time he delivered a coffee order to this exact table. With the pesky floorboard in his sights, he stubbed his toe on another floorboard. His tray of hot coffee shifted as he adjusted his balance. He steadied himself and inhaled deeply to calm his nerves, noticing that he had not spilled a single drop of coffee.

He took one more step to assert his presence at the wobbly, square, wooden table that sat perched against the window. A light rain fell outside, but the window remained relatively dry, allowing him to see people walking by in front of the soup kitchen across the street. These people scurried to their next destinations without paying a drop of attention to the fact that he had almost spilled hot coffee on his customers inside the building. In fact, most of these pedestrians didn't even look left or right to acknowledge that anything existed outside of their own self-absorption.

"One cappuccino," the barista announced.

A woman with wire-rimmed glasses raised a finger; she wore her hair in a bun held together with a pen, producing a first impression of intellect and curiosity. The barista handed the large mug to the woman, who thanked him with a nod and a smile.

"Two Americanos," the barista continued.

A woman with red lipstick and a man with a thin mustache raised their fingers. The barista reached over the mustached man to serve the woman first.

"And a cappuccino with an extra shot of espresso," the barista said.

A man in the corner raised his finger. His expression seemed smug, like he had ordered something more exceptional than his counterparts by adding an extra shot of espresso. Or maybe it was his half-unbuttoned shirt. Or the way he crossed one leg over the other. The barista couldn't pinpoint exactly what it was, but the man's aura bothered him. Regardless, he handed the drink to the man, who took the coffee and returned his attention to his counterparts without any acknowledgement of the barista's service.

"Double shot," Maxine said, adjusting the pen in her hair. "Nice move."

"It's what all the great French thinkers do," Donald replied, smiling with one side of his face, proud of his cultural understanding.

"Anything else I can get for you?" the barista asked, trying his best to suppress his annoyance with the group.

"Uh, no," Donald said, looping the handle of his coffee mug with his index finger.

He sipped his coffee slow, swishing the coffee around in his mouth elegantly to acquaint his palette with the roast of the bean. He smacked his lips twice to signify that he had sensed the coffee's origin and roasting style, looking upward to project an image of flavor contemplation. He dropped his face and shrugged, showing his friends that the coffee would pass, though it did not surpass his exquisite palate's expectations.

Donald had met these three friends recently. They had just moved to Portland from California after completing their master's program in art history. They joined a book group that met weekly at Quimby's. Donald had been in this particular book group for two years, but the group was mostly older people, a stark contrast to Donald's youthful age of 24. His new friends were the same age, and they sought Donald's expertise on the city of Portland. He finally felt needed. Appreciated, even. And they were smart. They discussed topics with a level of intellect that Donald craved. And he fed right into their conversations on a regular basis, projecting himself as a supreme intellectual being to his new social group.

"As I was saying," Donald said. "I just don't understand modern society. All of these teenagers walk around attached to their devices without really *seeing* the world around them."

He swirled his free hand around as he spoke to emphasize certain words.

"I completely agree with you, Donny," Cheston said, smoothing out his mustache. "Back when we were kids, we went outside. We hiked in the woods. We actually *spoke* to people."

"And it taught us to be independent thinkers," Donny said. "The modern young human is simply a follower. Uneducated in the ways of literature, society, and free thinking. They're trapped by their own existence."

"And it amazes me how quickly that transition has occurred," Maxine said. "Think about it; we only graduated from high school *six* years ago. And high schoolers today are so far removed from the level that our generation attained."

Donny smirked and rolled his eyes.

"What, Donny?" Maxine asked.

"The thought of high school being a major marker in a person's life just floors me," Donald said. "I mean, come on. Did we really *learn* anything in high school? Besides how to regurgitate text from a corporate book production company, of course."

Maxine sank back into her chair.

"I just don't see how our society deems the completion of high school as a true accomplishment," Donald continued. "Much less as a measure of intellect."

He sipped his coffee, allowing his point to sink in before progressing to his next point.

"I don't believe that people should be considered intelligent simply because they completed high school," Donald said. "I tend to want to associate myself with people who have at least completed their master's degree. I deem that degree as a base form of intellect."

The barista rolled his eyes as he walked by the table. He made eye contact with the girl in red lipstick. She smiled at the barista apologetically.

"I envy people that live in European society," Donald continued. "They just value education so much more than us Americans. The Italians, for example, can all speak more than three languages. The French transfer their intellect into high art, like Impressionist painting and exquisite culinary achievements. The Germans produce some of the most efficient and original engineering in the entire world. It's just such a culturally superior region by comparison."

He sipped his coffee slowly, methodically. He looked to Cheston, giving him an opportunity to interject an opinion or philosophical caveat before continuing on with his own. Cheston took the opening.

"Especially by comparison to other parts of the world," Cheston said.

"Oh, indeed," Donald said. "These poor people in the Middle East don't have access to education, much less any sense of culture. The concept of a truly intelligent person from the Middle East is almost laughable."

"It is well-known that great thoughts, concepts, and philosophies come from Europe," Maxine interjected. "And the United States, to some extent."

"And don't even get me started on the lack of intellect in Latin America," Donald said. "Those poor people probably can't do basic addition and subtraction, much less debate the intricacies of global philosophies."

The barista approached the table to collect empty mugs and ask for refills. Hearing Donald's comment, he stopped short. It resonated loudly within him. His brain fired. His nerves pulsed. His eyebrows narrowed.

He put his towel over his shoulder and clasped his hands together calmly, looking directly at Donald.

"Wow, man," the barista said. "You seem pretty well-educated."

Donald smiled, missing the sarcasm.

"Well, I suppose you could say that," Donald said. "I did earn my master's degree in the humanities at a private institution recently. I'm in the process of deciding whether or not to pursue my doctorate."

The barista nodded to feign approval.

"You also seem pretty well-travelled," the barista said. "Where have you been?"

Donald's confident facade faded, but he caught himself, projecting his chest to overcompensate for his difficulty with the question.

"You know," Donald said, "I've seen some fascinating

places in my life. I've learned a lot from my travels throughout southern Oregon, even as far north as Seattle."

The barista raised an eyebrow, condescendingly curious.

"I meant outside of the Pacific Northwest," the barista said. "Where else have you been?"

"I've studied other cultures and countries quite vigorously," Donald said.

The barista smiled, seeing straight through Donald's evasion.

"Have you ever been outside of the Pacific Northwest?" the barista asked.

Donald looked down at his coffee, swirling it around to stall for time. The barista crossed his arms, signifying impatience.

"No," Donald said. "No, I've never been outside of the country, or the Pacific Northwest."

The three friends at the table leaned forward in unison with shocked expressions on their faces.

"Donny!" the girl in red lipstick shouted. "You've never left the country?"

"But you always talk about other cultures and countries like you've lived there for years," Maxine said.

Donald's face turned red. Feelings of rage swirled through his pulse. Insecurity dug into his nerves. He directed his glare toward the barista, who stood firmly near the table.

"What do you even know about intellect?" Donald said. "You're just serving coffee. You don't understand the complexities of the world."

The barista smiled, daring Donald to challenge him. And

he did.

"What's your highest level of education, you peasant?" Donald spouted.

The barista's smile widened. He ducked his head to hide his emerging laughter.

"Look man," the barista said. "I graduated from high school two years ago. I'm a student at Portland College right now. So, on paper, I'm probably not as educated as you are. But I do know some things. First, I know that you don't know anything about me, and for you to assume that you do is a reflection on your own lack of a specific type of intellect: street smarts. While you've been isolated in your hometown and your way of thinking, I've experienced more than most people will in a lifetime. I was born and raised in Mexico. My family moved to Brazil when I was five to be with my dad's family, and we navigated the *favelas* with skill. After my father was killed, we sought asylum in Turkey before finally entering into the eligibility window for immigration to the United States."

Donald opened his mouth to speak, but the barista cut him off.

"I speak Spanish, Portuguese, Italian, Arabic, and English. I've navigated the streets of Mexico, the slums of Brazil, the back alleys of Turkey, and the center of Portland. I've hustled on the streets to get enough money to afford school in four different countries. I've reasoned my way out of more life-or-death scenarios than you can imagine. I've spent more time debating the intricacies of philosophy while watching soccer on ancient television screens than you could ever discuss in a college classroom. I've spoken with more ethic groups than you even know exist. I've seen the incredible achievements of cultures, religions, and individuals across three continents. When it comes to intellect, a person needs to pair education with experience and compassion, three attributes that I take pride in cultivating."

Donald wanted to refute the barista's statements. He wanted to save his own image of superiority, but he couldn't find words to throw at the barista. Instead, his mouth remained open, dumbfounded. He looked to his friends for support, but there was none to give. They simply looked down at their coffees, outmatched in intellect. Donald refocused his attention to the barista, whose focus had never wavered.

"So, you tell me," the barista said. "What is intellect?"

THE CHESS PLAYER

Fatinah adjusted her hijab as she waited patiently for the train. A light rain drizzled from overcast clouds, but she stood underneath a tree, which blocked most of the moisture from reaching her.

The train approached and she walked through its doors, finding a seat that faced inward. She liked these seats; they allowed her to see most people on the train. Fatinah enjoyed watching people interact. She enjoyed seeing different types of people, and the train was definitely a place to widen one's perspective.

A woman with red lipstick and a man with a thin mustache sat next to her, leaving one seat between them to create the illusion of privacy and division. They were discussing the current state of politics in the Middle East. Fatinah smiled to herself as they spouted off biased, American stereotypes about the Middle East; they discussed these inaccuracies with astounding confidence.

An older white man sat across the aisle from Fatinah. She watched him discreetly as he placed his backpack and walking stick on the seat next to him. Then, his eyes shifted to explore his surroundings. He noticed Fatinah and his eyes lifted to her headscarf. Aside from a quick eyebrow raise, his face remained neutral, hiding his internal fear of an expressive Muslim person on his train.

Fatinah smiled to project peace and happiness. She was well aware of most Americans' fears of Muslims. Some of that stemmed from the attacks on the World Trade Center in 2001, of course. But Fatinah attributed most of that fear to the way in which American media portrayed Muslims and discussed the Middle East in general. It depicted Middle Eastern people and culture in a negative light that had stoked fear in an entire generation of Americans.

Fatinah was a young graduate student at Portland College when the planes struck the Twin Towers in New York City. She felt fear like most Americans did at the time. Fear of the unknown. Fear that there would be more attacks. Fear that the United States wasn't as safe as it told itself it was. Some of her understanding about the situation came from her college courses and discussions, but most of her education surrounding the issue came through her own experience.

Walking down the street in 2001 felt dangerous. Not because she was afraid of another attack, but because she sensed hatred in other people. They looked at Fatinah's hijab and immediately associated her with terrorists. They saw her Arab ethnicity and instantly viewed her as an enemy. They saw her outward display of Islam and feared her very existence. People would walk across the street to avoid being close to her. She was pulled from every airport security line she walked through, no matter how meticulous she was about following the newly-imposed travel guidelines.

Now, Fatinah largely went unnoticed. Sure, she received the occasional eyebrow raise from a xenophobic old man on the train, but people mostly left her alone. Oftentimes, she even felt invisible, only broken up by people looking at her headscarf as something new and different. The feeling of invisibility didn't feel good, but it was a significant improvement from the constant negative attention she received in the wake of the attacks on the Twin Towers.

This feeling of invisibility wasn't new to Fatinah. Growing up in Egypt, she often felt like no one noticed her; partly because of her gender, partly because of her economic status. Fatinah came from an impoverished family in Cairo. Her father was a modest educator at a local Islamic school, and her mother maintained the household. When Fatinah was a child, she walked to and from school, navigating the winding maze of Cairo's streets. Eventually, she used her gift of language to sell counterfeit goods after school to make a little extra cash for her family.

She was quite good at using her irresistible child eyes and advanced vocabulary to convince afternoon tea drinkers to purchase jewelry they didn't need. Fatinah saw street sales as a strategic game. As an invisible member of society, she observed and absorbed. Fatinah knew where old men went after work, where old women went to escape their husbands for a while, and where the older kids went to avoid their parents. And she stationed herself in the most advantageous locations to make it look like *they* were coming to *her*. She played into their egos.

Fatinah was 11 when her family immigrated to the United States. Her family had a relative who lived in Portland, so they eventually found their way to the Rose City. Fatinah loved the new environment, but it was difficult to make friends. And school didn't come as easy to her as it did in Egypt, especially language classes, like English. She had to learn to write from left to right instead of right to left. She had to learn an entirely new alphabet. She was also the only one wearing a headscarf. Kids in middle school made fun of her, but eventually she came to see her hijab as a symbol of pride in her heritage. And her street smarts, refined in the alleyways of Cairo, gave her the tools to navigate her way through high school and into college.

The chess boards in Pioneer Courthouse Square looked old and a little run down, but Fatinah gravitated toward them. She would stand and watch old men play for hours, learning their strategies, their tendencies, and their egos. One day, an old man invited her to sit down and play. And she did.

And she won.

Fatinah's apartment was near Pioneer Square during her undergraduate years at Portland College, and she found her way to those chess tables every day. And she continued that tradition into her graduate school years.

In fact, she was playing chess at those tables on the

morning of the attacks on the World Trade Center.

Playing chess gave her a feeling of purpose. A feeling that she wasn't invisible, at least for a brief moment. When two or three people gathered to watch her play another old white man, she felt like a champion. Because she almost always won.

And today was no different. Fatinah stepped off the train and walked across the bricks in the plaza. She loved the view of skyscrapers towering over the open public area. Sometimes she walked even slower just to take in the people, absorb the city, until she made her way to the chess tables on the other side of the square.

Fatinah stood against a street sign post and watched as two older gentlemen played into a near stalemate. Mentally, she critiqued their moves, predicting their next steps with uncanny accuracy. No one noticed her standing there, of course.

A middle-aged white woman walked along the sidewalk carrying a large coffee in a paper cup, talking loudly on her phone. She stopped near the chess tables, speaking as if no one else could hear her.

"I can't believe it," the woman shouted. "I mean, they're just letting these homeless people destroy the city. They're everywhere. Begging, sleeping, standing, looking through the trash. It's terrible."

She paused and listened to the person on the other end.

"I know!" the woman shouted into the phone. "They're such an eyesore. I just can't stand looking at them."

The woman took a sip of coffee and continued her power

walk. Fatinah rolled her eyes at the woman's conversation. The living conditions of people in her old neighborhood in Cairo were far better than the conditions of many homeless people in Portland. And all of the families in their neighborhood helped each other out, and so did their local mosque, rather than looking at people in need as an inconvenience.

A group of high school students followed shortly behind the woman. They wore brand name shoes and sweatshirts and laughed loudly at each other.

"I'm pissed my mom got me *these* shoes for my birthday," one boy said. "I wanted the retros, but my mom said they were too expensive. I mean, come on."

Fatinah laughed audibly. The shoes on the kid's feet were worth more than her current daily wage, which would feed a family for a month in her old neighborhood in Cairo.

"Yeah, well at least she also got you a new car for your birthday," one girl said. "My dad only got me a *used* car."

Fatinah's laugh grew stronger. Families in her old neighborhood, even in her new circle of friends, had to work for years to afford a used car, much less maintain it.

The students crossed the street after the train passed, and their conversation faded from earshot. But two college boys approached through the square, giving Fatinah another chance to listen in on ridiculous problems.

"I can't believe they were out of chocolate chip breakfast muffins at the coffee shop," one boy said.

"You could have gotten blueberry," the other boy said.

"Blueberry? No way," the boy said. "Now I'm going to

have to go hungry all morning."

Fatinah's eyebrows narrowed with scorn. These wealthy kids knew nothing of hunger. They had never felt the pain that accompanied an entire day without food, and not because of one's choice to forgo a disliked flavor, but the hunger that struck when there was literally no food to be had. Or the hunger that came from fasting during Ramadan in the summer, when the days were long and hot. Or the hunger that came from wanting to be seen, to strive for more, knowing that there was a ceiling.

Her scorn at the boys' ridiculous conversation bubbled into more audible laughter; her mother taught her that laughter was the best medicine.

Finally, the game between the two old men finished. One old man stood and shook the winner's hand, and then strolled into the square, dissipating into the crowd. The winner sat at the chess table, looking around for another challenger. When no one approached the seat, Fatinah took three steps toward her next opponent, who greeted her with kind eyes. His white face was wrinkled and weathered, blending in with his gray moustache. He wore a hat that looked like it was a 1940s original. He motioned for Fatinah to sit.

"Well, hello there, my dear," the old man said. "Would you care to play a game of chess with an old fella?"

"I'd love to," Fatinah said.

The old man reached across the table and shook Fatinah's hand.

"I'm Paul," he said.

"Fatinah."

"Pleasure to meet ya," Paul said.

He looked up at her hijab.

"Say, I like your headscarf," Paul said. "The color really brings out your eyes."

Fatinah smiled. One of those genuine smiles that started in the heart and worked its way up.

"Thank you, sir," Fatinah said. "I like your hat."

Paul looked up without moving his head.

"This old thing?" he said. "I've had this since I was a young man. It's old, like me, but it sure does have some character."

They both smiled and laughed. Paul set up the board and looked politely at Fatinah.

"Have you played much chess, my dear?" Paul asked.

"I sure have," Fatinah said. "I love the game."

"Well, I must say, I'm pretty good," Paul said. "But I also need you to know that I'm not going to take it easy on you even though we just met. Would you care to go first?"

"Winner's choice," Fatinah said.

Paul smiled kindly and waved his hand to indicate that Fatinah had the first move.

Fatinah moved a black pawn on the left side of the board. Paul nearly mimicked the move with his white pawn. Their pawns danced for a while until Fatinah moved a bishop toward the right side of the board, and then she moved a knight nearby. She liked to move a few major pieces out early and let them wait. She liked to have her major attacking points ready to strike when her opponent would least expect it. She allowed her opponent to capture most of her pawns to give them a sense of accomplishment. Just like her sales strategy as a kid in Cairo, Fatinah played to her opponent's ego.

She moved her rook along the left side, taking out Paul's knight, and then she moved her knight along the left side, indicating an attack. Paul took the bait. He saw an opening to take Fatinah's black knight out with his queen. Feigning defeat, Fatinah slowly moved her hand toward her bishop and slid it across the board to capture the white queen. On her next move, she took her other knight out of hiding and moved him to the left. Paul captured the knight with his last remaining bishop.

Fatinah smiled, knowing that Paul had played right into her plan. No one could resist capturing a knight. Fatinah reached toward her back line and slowly pushed her black queen down the board, taking out Paul's bishop. His eyes widened.

"Checkmate," Fatinah said.

THE WALLFLOWER

Julia's pen scribbled methodically as she copied the notes on the board. Her math teacher was explaining a calculus problem. His notes were everywhere, like his brain had exploded onto the board with no concept of executive functioning. Julia did her best to turn his notes into a workable format with some strategy so she could reference them while she completed her homework, and then when she studied for her test. It was a good thing she played chess; that sense of strategy gave her enough foresight to recognize the need for coherent notes. Once she had solved the problem and checked her teacher's notes for confirmation, Julia proceeded to doodle in the margins of her notebook.

Her teacher was asking for volunteers to explain their problem-solving processes, and Julia kept her hand down as usual. School tended to come easy to Julia, but she hadn't raised her hand since probably seventh grade. As the only junior in a room full of seniors in Advanced Calculus, she wasn't going to start today. She still wondered why she was nominated for the honor society. Sure, she got perfect grades, but it wasn't like she tried hard in school. She just did her work and turned in her stuff.

Thankfully, the bell rang before her math teacher could cold-call another so-called volunteer. She tossed her notebook into her backpack and calmly made her way into the sea of student traffic. Freshmen weaved nervously between full-grown seniors, while sophomores did their best to tread water. Juniors had the potential to stand out. Occasionally a popular junior would get a shout out from a senior across the hallway, but only the popular ones. Not Julia.

But she almost preferred it that way. In some ways, moving invisibly through high school had its benefits. No one had a need to talk trash about you behind your back. No one expected much out of you, so you were less prone to failure. And it allowed you to move effortlessly through the insanity of passing period.

Julia moved into the center of the hallway. She looked to her left and the sea of students parted, creating an unobstructed pathway for God himself: Devon Williams. He walked slowly. He strolled with such confidence. His hand raised to high-five a football teammate, who reveled in the glory of being associated with an icon like Devon. All of the girls clamored to get closer to him, but stopped before entering his pathway, like an invisible velvet rope protected him from his flocking fans.

Devon Williams was the coolest kid in school, without question. He was the star quarterback on the football team, and he was in the middle of a record-setting season that was full of unbelievable highlights. He was the point guard on the basketball team, an academic all-star, and the overwhelming favorite to win Homecoming King again in a few weeks. Julia watched as he casually adjusted his backpack strap and his white letterman's jacket, which contrasted perfectly with his flawless dark skin.

Then she watched as Devon continued walking directly toward her. Julia realized she was standing in his path. She started to panic; sweat started to form on her brow. He was approaching quickly. What would he say to her? What was *she* going to say back? He was four steps away, smiling, with a purpose.

He was so close. Time stopped. Julia watched as his smile floated toward her, calling her into his presence.

Devon slowed down, almost hovered. He was about to stop right in front of Julia.

And then he walked right on by her. Not even a glance in her direction. So much for invisibility having its benefits.

Julia shook her shoulders, causing her body to unlock from its temporary love-struck trance. She moved through the maze of hallways until she found her safe zone: the band room. Third period was band class, and she needed to release some emotions on the drums.

"Ms. Martinez," her band teacher said. "How are you this morning?"

"I'm fine, Mrs. Stevens," she said. "I just really want to

rock on the drums by myself today, if that's alright."

Mrs. Stevens smiled. Julia was the best drummer in the school. She had held the first spot on the drum line since she set foot into school as a freshman, taking to the snap of the snare drum in particular, though she could have been first place in any drum selection she wanted. Mrs. Stevens would let Julia do whatever she wanted, as long as she kept playing drums at such a high level.

"Of course it's alright, Julia," Mrs. Stevens said. "You can head into the drum booth and mess around on the set today while we work on tuning some of these flutes out here."

Julia smiled and headed into the relatively sound-proof drum booth. She pulled her drumsticks out of her backpack, sat on the stool, kicked the bass, and let her drumsticks fly.

I can't believe Devon just walked by me and didn't even notice I was there, Julia thought. *I've had, like, six classes with him since we were freshmen.*

Her head started to nod with more intent. Her braids flew around her head, knocking into her shoulders with force, but she didn't notice. Or care. She was in the zone.

Julia met Devon on the first day of freshman year. He sat next to her in their advisory class. He leaned over to her while the teacher was talking and introduced himself. She shook his hand nervously and felt butterflies. But they started to run in different circles almost immediately. He was an athlete who started hanging out with the junior football players and the flocks of sophomore girls that threw themselves at him. Meanwhile, Julia knew she was a band geek, one of those kids who was good at school, but didn't really fit in with a crew.

She thought this year would be different; she had English class with Devon. The first day of English class, she sat next to him and greeted him in a semi-flirtatious way. He just nodded and turned around to talk to one of his basketball buddies. Her stomach sank, reinforcing the fact that she was invisible. Devon didn't even know who she was. She felt so stupid for having such a crush on someone who didn't even know she existed.

Her hands flew around the drum set with ferocity. Her braids waved in rhythm with her body rock. Julia's drumsticks had a mind of their own. Sweat started to bead on her brow. And then Mrs. Stevens opened the drum booth and waved her arms wildly, snapping Julia out of her trance.

"Julia, class is over," Mrs. Stevens said.

"Already?" Julia asked. "I feel like I've only been here for a few minutes."

"That happens when you're focused," Mrs. Stevens said. "But it's been 45 minutes. Time for your next class, my dear."

Julia slid her drumsticks into her backpack and emerged from the booth, braving the chaos of the hallways during passing period. She made her way to English class, feeling much better after a lengthy drum session.

She walked into the classroom and she took her unofficial assigned seat in the second row. Since she was early, she took out a book from her backpack and started reading, knowing that no one else was going to make conversation with her.

Devon walked in and sat next to her in his unofficial assigned seat. Julia had sat next to him for almost two months and they hadn't had a single interaction. She just felt so nervous to say anything. He was in a social class above her, and that's how it was always going to be.

She reached for her backpack to replace her book. When she opened it, her drumsticks fell out. As she picked them up, she felt an overwhelming sense of purpose, of true confidence. She felt visible. Julia sat up and looked at Devon.

"Hey, Devon," Julia said. "How come we never talk?"

Devon's head shook involuntarily. He opened his mouth to say something, but he stuttered.

"We're two months into school and we sit by each other every day," Julia continued. "I feel like we should know each other by now."

Devon's coolness had returned, at least on the surface.

"Julia Martinez, I know who you are," Devon said. "Yo, you kill it on the snare drum at halftime."

THE HOMECOMING KING

Devon gripped his backpack straps as he walked down the hallway. He only had a few more minutes until the bell rang; he hated being late. The massive crowd of students hanging around their lockers like they had nowhere else to be made him anxious. He didn't understand how they could act so relaxed.

As he dodged his way through the crowd, one of his football teammates shouted.

"Devon! What's good?"

Devon looked at his teammate, feigned a smile, and reached over another student to high five him. He wanted to stop and ask his teammate about the math test, but he didn't want to be late, and he had to walk all the way across the school. And this giant group of girls was just standing in his way. *What could possibly be so interesting that they're willing to be late to class for?*

And then he saw her: Julia Martinez.

She stood in the middle of the hallway looking so casual, so calm, so cool. Maybe it was the way her braids draped over her shoulder. Or maybe it was the style she brought to school every day: effortlessly edgy. It could have been her brains. Or the way she rocked the drums. But those eyes. They were filled with such mystery, such kindness. He felt like she was too good for him.

Julia made him nervous, which was weird for Devon. He felt so in control on the football field, the basketball court, writing an essay, taking a test, answering questions in the classroom, and even performing at assemblies. But Julia was different. He had planned to talk to her every day in English class, now that they finally had a class together. But every time he tried, he froze up. He would overthink what he wanted to say, play out all the what-if scenarios, hesitate, and then the moment would pass him by.

And there she was, just standing alone with confidence. Maybe now was the time to talk to her. Finally.

He set his path toward her. He planned his icebreaker line, but didn't like it, so he changed his mind. Then he switched it again. And then he was four steps away from her. Julia looked at Devon, and he locked eyes with her for a moment. As he took his approaching step, panic tackled him like a linebacker. He walked right by Julia without saying a word.

What was I thinking? Devon thought. *I froze up again!*

His mind raced with self-criticism as he entered the advanced chemistry classroom. He sat near the front as he usually did. Devon wanted to be present for each and every class in order to earn the best grades possible. But today, he wasn't into it. He couldn't stop focusing on his cowardice; he didn't understand why he couldn't just *talk* to Julia.

The chemistry teacher stood at the front of the room and droned on about molecules. Devon's mind drifted. Usually when it drifted, he thought about football, basketball, even filmmaking. But not today. Today, he was focused on self-doubt.

"Alright," the teacher bellowed. "Close your books, get out a pencil. It's time for a pop quiz."

Devon's hands began to shake. He felt sweat begin to bead on his forehead. A surprise attack by the chemistry teacher. *Damn.*

The teacher placed the pop quiz on each student's desk. Devon grabbed his, flipped through it, and stopped for a minute to plan his strategy. Question two looked promising, but question three presented some problems. And Devon's focus wasn't all in. His pencil flew through the test, half-inspired by academic achievement, and half by anxiety.

"Alright," the teacher said, "put your pencils down. Trade your quiz with a partner, and that partner will grade your answers as I read them out loud."

A kid in the back of the room chuckled, intending to give his friend a better grade than he deserved.

"And be honest," the teacher said. "I'll re-grade these later."

The kid in the back of the room let his smirk drop to a frown.

As the teacher gave the answer to each question, Devon

looked over at his own paper to see how he was scoring, but the view was difficult to pull off smoothly. Finally, his partner returned the paper to Devon, who eagerly snatched it from her hand.

I missed a question? Devon thought. *Mom's gonna kill me.*

His heart started to race, but he smiled calmly to project an image of achievement and composure. He knew that missing one question would earn him a less-than-perfect score, and enough less-than-perfect scores added up to a less-than-perfect final grade, which led to something less than an Ivy League school.

And that was Devon's goal: Harvard, Yale, Brown. Even Columbia would suffice. That had been his goal since he started school in kindergarten. To earn an academic and athletic scholarship to one of the best schools in the country. Or it had been his mom's goal. Or maybe a little bit of both.

This goal didn't seem to impact Devon in grade school. The end result seemed too far away. As he moved into middle school, he realized that he loved playing basketball and football. And he recognized that he was pretty good. But the move to high school shook him. Grades finally counted. Scouts started calling. And he found more options to pursue, like filmmaking. But these interests weren't acceptable in his mother's eyes. *Making videos won't get you into Harvard,* she'd say. As a sophomore, the fear of failure began to grip Devon. And it tightened its grip with each minor setback: a missed question on a quiz, a simple mistake with a homework problem, an errant pass on the field. These missteps didn't happen often, but when they did, they paralyzed him.

And he didn't want to misstep with Julia. The fear of failure, of rejection, could paralyze him from succeeding in English class, and potentially on the football field as well. And it was that fear of failure that caused him to cruise by Julia in the hallway.

But courage still had a grasp on Devon. When he entered English class at the beginning of the school year, he noticed Julia had already claimed a seat. And he strategically claimed a seat next to her. He knew that this would provide an opening to talk to her, to break the ice, yet remain protected instead of vulnerable, like a running back with a blocker.

And then two months passed without a word. Julia rarely looked in his direction. Devon was starting to think that she didn't even know he existed. He was confident enough to start up a conversation with every other person in the class, but the girl sitting next to him left Devon frozen.

With homecoming approaching, Devon knew he needed to ask a date. He had heard rumors that people were going to vote for him as Homecoming King for another year, so this date had to be willing to roll with the evening. And Devon knew Julia would be the best date in the entire world.

But how could he ask her? He didn't even know her. He had actually never spoken to her, at least not that he could remember.

And then he heard it; two drumsticks hit the floor and produced an unmistakable sound. Devon looked toward the drumsticks. As Julia reached to pick them up, their eyes met. Julia sat up in her seat with poise and confidence; she looked at Devon. Her kind eyes seemed to see Devon's heart.

"Hey, Devon," Julia said. "How come we never talk?"

Devon's head shook involuntarily. He couldn't believe she had actually talked to him. He had planned this moment in his brain hundreds of times, but executing the play in a game time scenario was a different element.

"We're two months into school and we sit by each other every day," Julia continued. "I feel like we should know each other by now."

Devon panicked. She had just exposed his weakness, his cowardice. But then again, how cool was it that she had the courage to do that? *Who is this girl?*

"Julia Martinez, I know who you are," Devon said. "Yo, you kill it on the snare drum at halftime."

THE GROOM

Luke peered through the doorway and looked into the church. Every pew seemed packed. He recognized some people: family members he hadn't seen since he was a little kid, friends from college that he hadn't talked to in a while, some of his parents' friends that he didn't really know. Everybody was dressed well for the occasion. Luke didn't dress up that often. In fact, the last time he wore something this fancy was probably for a homecoming dance in high school.

As he continued to scan the crowd for familiar faces, he saw more and more people that he hadn't seen before. His fiancé's extended family, maybe. Her friends from college that lived in different states, possibly. Her coworkers that he had heard about but never actually met, likely.

Luke felt his hands begin to shake. His breath started to quicken. These unknown guests made him nervous. They were about to become an interconnected piece of his life, of his existence. And yet he didn't know them. He had no idea how they would influence him, or even *if* they would influence him. The thought of the unknown pushed against him. Luke's vision pushed inward, creating black spots in his peripheral view.

He closed the door to his dressing room and leaned against it to calm his nerves. Closing his eyes, he breathed in through his nose slowly, and then exhaled through his mouth. He looked around the corner and saw his groomsmen sitting on couches, laughing, and sneaking sips of whiskey in paper cups.

Luke envied them today; all they had to do was show up, stand there, and enjoy themselves. Their lives would not change significantly after today; all they would be left with was a memory of a fun party and a new addition to their friend's life.

But not Luke. His life would be altered forever.

He didn't wrestle with doubt. He knew that his fiancé, Katie, was the one. She was smart, brilliant even. Katie held a high-level job that she genuinely enjoyed, came from a fun family, and maintained a set of values that was in some ways equivalent to Luke's own set of values, and in some ways challenged his assumptions. And, of course, she was beautiful. The kind of beautiful that seemed effortless, timeless.

No, Luke didn't have cold feet. But he was nervous. He just wasn't sure where his nerves were coming from.

Taking one more glance at his groomsmen, Luke turned

and left the room. He just needed to walk. To breathe some fresh air. The candle smoke and church incense made him feel nauseous, and the cramped dressing room grew smaller by the minute.

He took a step into the entryway of the church, but he saw too many semi-familiar faces. Faces he didn't want to interact with until after the wedding. Luke pivoted and walked down the back hallway. Turning a corner, he saw a door that led to the outside world. To fresh air. He turned the doorknob and pushed. A thin layer of fresh air entered the hallway, immediately lifting Luke's spirits. But briefly.

"Luke!" a voice shouted from somewhere in the dark hallway.

He shut the door and peered into the shadows from the corridor he had just walked through.

"Luke!" the familiar voice said again. "You're not running away, are you?"

Luke's father emerged into the light, smiling at his own joke. Luke smiled too.

"Of course not, Dad," Luke said. "I just needed some fresh air."

"I understand that, son," Dad said. "Mind if I join you?"

Luke hesitated. He really just wanted to be alone with his own thoughts. But he couldn't turn down this offer out of respect for the day.

"I don't mind at all," Luke said.

Luke pushed the door open and a plume of fresh air rejuvenated him again. The bright, overcast sky caused his eyes to recoil, a stark contrast to the darkness of the church corridors. A light mist fell from the clouds. The mist coated the streets in a thin layer of water. It suppressed the raw smells of the street and replaced it with a renewed sense of nature. Rain had a way of doing that: resetting the city's attitude.

Luke and his father turned right and walked down the sidewalk, away from the church's front entrance. Cars rolled by, glistening after the light rain shower. Headlights created contrasting shadows on brick walls as cars prepared for the winter's early nightfall. Luke shoved his hands in his pockets to fight off the biting chill.

"You doing alright, Luke?" Dad said.

Luke looked down at his shoes. Water droplets beaded on the false shine of the leather.

"Kind of," Luke said. "I'm just nervous, I guess."

"You should be," Dad said.

Luke turned toward his father and lifted an eyebrow.

"I should?"

"Of course," Dad said. "You're about to get married. It's a whole new chapter in your life that you've never had any experience with."

"I guess you're right," Luke said.

"But you'll be fine," Dad continued. "No person is fully ready for marriage. You can't be. You're joining your life together with another human being. Another family who looks at the world differently, has different traditions that you do, and who will bring perspectives to your life that you don't recognize."

"I love Katie, Dad, I know I do," Luke said. "I just hope

this whole thing works and keeps us both happy, you know? I don't want to lose myself."

Luke's father smiled.

"I'm glad to hear you say that, son," Dad said. "It's important that you stay *you*, and continue to strive to be the best version of yourself. And it's important that Katie has that mindset too."

Luke remained silent. He counted each square in the sidewalk that his foot touched.

"How do you balance the whole *family* thing?" Luke asked.

"What do you mean?" Dad said.

"Well, I don't know how I'm going to balance the old and the new," Luke said. "I love our family's traditions and the way we do things. And Katie loves the way her family does things. How do we balance that?"

Luke's father smiled and placed his hand on Luke's shoulder.

"Families have fought that same battle for thousands of years, son," Dad said. "The way I see it, you're starting your *own* family. A new family. You can take the traditions that you liked from our family and the ones that Katie liked from her family and blend them together to create something new. You just have to prioritize your *new* family that you're going to create here in about 20 minutes."

Luke looked at his father, understanding what he said, but not fully grasping the concept. Luke's father read his son's eyes and continued with the thought.

"Take this building across the street," Dad said. "It's an old brick building. Probably built in the early 1900s as a warehouse. Over time, the city around the warehouse changed. The city's needs changed. The city's interests changed. So, the building had to adapt to its new surroundings. It joined with a new contractor who blended the building's old features that still had value: exposed brick, classic iron beams, wide open space inside. And that contractor added some new flavor and gave the building a new purpose. He pulled the best features from the traditional building and paired it with the best features of modern architecture to create something new."

Luke placed his hand on his father's shoulder and smiled.

Their walk around the block had returned them to the church's entrance. The crowd was seated, so Luke and his father snuck through the main entrance without being bothered by guests. Luke's brother met them in the hallway with an empty paper cup.

"We thought you ran away," his brother said. "It's not too late."

Luke laughed and punched his brother's arm.

"No, man. I'm good."

Luke's father looked at his watch.

"Well, boys," Dad said. "It's time."

THE DECEASED

Rain fell heavily on the pavement, creating puddles in the old North Portland sidewalks. Drains were blocked with fall leaves, so puddles lined the curbs. As cars pulled up to the church, people in their elegant clothes navigated the puddles to keep their shoes from getting wet.

The outdoor courtyard and entryway into the church appeared eerily empty, but inside, people packed into pews and filled the standing room in the back by the fountain of holy water. Even the choir loft was full.

People buzzed through the crowd to find people they recognized, their closest point of contact with the family. It helped those who were not quite as close to the deceased to send their condolences to immediate members of the family. Choruses of "I'm so sorry" and "How are you holding up?" echoed through the church.

Outside, six pallbearers carried a dark wood casket

through the rain. They walked slowly, ignoring the drops that doused their suit jackets. They stepped nearly in unison. Six middle-aged men, clean shaven, freckled white skin, and dark brown hair, neatly combed. Not twins, but imprints. Six hands grasped the casket handles. Six pairs of eyes shed slow, controlled tears. Six brothers carrying their mother.

The brothers carried the casket up the cement steps and entered the church. As they passed through the entrance area, they were greeted by a large photograph of their mother's smiling face, her wrinkles defined and elegant. Below the portrait, it read: *Margaret Cathleen Sullivan.*

The sons passed the photograph, holding back tears, masking their sadness with flexed jaws and heads held high. They walked methodically down the aisle; a hymn rang out from the piano. As they approached the front of the church, they turned and placed the casket on its stand, which was surrounded by flowers.

As if orchestrated by a conductor, the crowd stood at the same moment as the priest, who took a few steps toward the crowd and greeted them in prayer. He began a traditional funeral mass, in which members of the family read from the Old Testament, New Testament, a few selected Psalms, and a guest hymn by a granddaughter. Members of the crowd who sat close to each family member congratulated each speaker in a conciliatory kind of way.

Then, the priest introduced the main speaker for the ceremony: Margaret's youngest son, Michael, who would give the official eulogy.

Michael stood from his seat in the front pew. He gripped

his speech notes so hard that the sheets of paper shook. He inhaled deeply through his nose, and exhaled through his mouth to calm himself as much as he could. When he reached the base of the altar, he bowed, and then made his way to the lectern.

He placed three sheets of paper on the podium, planted his feet, bent his knees, and faced the crowd. He breathed ritualistically one more time to calm himself. *If I mess this up, Mom is gonna kill me*, Michael thought.

He locked eyes with the clock in the back of the room and began his speech, a speech he had practiced so many times in the last three days that he probably didn't even need his notes.

"Thank you all for coming today," Michael began. "It means the world to my brothers and I to have you all here to support our mother in the same way that she has supported so many of us."

His gaze on the clock tightened as he fought back the first wave of tears.

"Somehow, I was chosen to summarize my mother's life story," Michael continued. "Eight decades of perfection brought to you all in three minutes. I guess it's because I'm the youngest and my older brothers can still tell me what to do, otherwise they'll beat me up."

The crowd released a slight chuckle, sadness and tension released with laughter. *Always start with a joke to loosen up the crowd*, Michael thought. He breathed deeply again to refocus his purpose.

"Margaret Cathleen Sullivan was born in Portland just before the Second World War. She was born into a world of economic depression, fear of changing governments, and fear of war. Born into a time when people didn't know what the future would hold, and, quite frankly, if there would even be a future at all."

The silence of the church felt heavy as he paused. He fixed his attention on the clock, wishing he could at least hear the clock ticking, or the gears turning. But all he felt was silence.

"And into that world of fear came a bright hope for the future: my mother, Margaret. Her father left to fight in the War in the Pacific, leaving a wife and three daughters behind, never to see them again. Margaret's mother raised three girls on her own, working three jobs to support her girls. When Margaret was old enough, she went to school, right here, in fact. The nuns provided free schooling for Margaret and her two sisters, and they sent the girls home with food for dinner every night, knowing how much the family needed this simple act of kindness."

Michael unlocked his focus on the clock and turned his head toward the priests that lined the space behind him. He gave them a nod of gratitude, and they returned with nods of acknowledgement, not for themselves, but for those who came before them.

"After my mother graduated from high school, she was encouraged to find a husband and become a homemaker, a notion that she gleefully rebelled against, opting to go to college instead. At a college just up the street from us, she earned her degree in nursing, a vocation that she would dedicate the next 35 year of her life to serving."

Michael fumbled through his notes until he could

effectively grab the first page and turn it to the second. He hadn't looked at his notes once, but it was comforting to know they were there.

"Margaret served as a trauma nurse high in the hills of Portland, helping the wounded, the frightened, and the dying get through the most difficult day in their entire lives. And she did this with grace. I'm sure she had days that were tough enough to make her want to quit. I'm sure she had days that made her cry with rage, rebuking the God that she so adamantly worshipped. And I'm sure she had days that haunted her for her entire life. And she did so with poise, never letting her anger and frustration make her bitter toward the world. Actually, it made her appreciate the world and the people in it more and more each day."

A lump started to well inside Michael's throat. He took a sip of water to force the tears and emotions back down, emotions he couldn't release until the speech was complete.

"At the age of 25, she married a dashing young Irish dock worker named Sean Sullivan, and they married shortly thereafter. Sean and Margaret had six boys, all of whom are here today, and all of whom were raised to become upstanding members of the Portland community. Except for Brian; we all know he's a loser. Sorry, Mom."

He cracked a smile and looked upward, acknowledging his mom's presence, knowing she would laugh at his jab toward Brian's altruistic success.

"Our mother and father raised us to respect people, to help our community, stand up for what's right, and to find the best in every situation. And the six of us Sullivan boys have instilled those same values onto our own kids, Margaret's 12 grandchildren."

Michael wanted to look at his own daughters, but he knew that he would melt if he made eye contact with them, so he strengthened his hold on the clock. Two minutes had already passed; he was way behind schedule for his three-minute speech.

"And Margaret didn't just tell us that we had to respect others, respect ourselves, and respect the community. She showed it with her actions. She dressed up every day and represented herself well, even on Sunday trips to the grocery store down the block. Even though she was a nurse and served Portland Monday through Friday, she still volunteered at soup kitchens, church events, school fundraisers, youth sports leagues, neighborhood clean-ups, and free clinics. It would have been easy for her to just kick her feet up and say she'd done enough, but she didn't. The world needed too much help."

If I can make it through the next section without breaking down, I'll be fine.

"When a neighborhood kid didn't have a good home to go to after school, she made sure they came over for dinner. When a neighbor was having a hard time making rent, she found a way to get them money. When a homeless person asked for help, she didn't give them money; she brought them here to church to give them purpose and a second chance. When us kids were having a bad day, she always knew the right thing to say to put things in perspective. And she always did these things with that signature Margaret Sullivan smile."

Michael smiled as he thought about his mother's own expression of happiness, of gratitude. The way her eyes squinted and creased on the edges. The way her nose wrinkled as she watched her boys knock each other around while they cleaned up after dinner. He knew she was smiling now, fully at peace. With that thought in his mind, an unusual calm enveloped Michael. Somehow, he knew it would be fine.

"As she got older, she often reflected on the city of Portland itself. We would take walks and she would point out things that used to be there, and the people that used to live in the house on the corner, that house that was torn down and is now a chain store. We'd drive downtown and she'd lament the rising skyline, comparing it to the simpler times of her youth. But she also acknowledged that as a city grows, it must change. It has to evolve with the times and with the people that it has helped to raise. She once told me that even though the city of her youth isn't here anymore, the echoes of that city will never leave, especially if you know where to look."

His eyes squinted as he rubbed the back of his neck, as if the truth in his own words finally made sense to him.

"I think that was her way of telling me that she wasn't going to be with us much longer. And she was right. Even though the Margaret that we knew is no longer with us, Margaret will never leave us. The echoes of Margaret's impact are right here in this room, within all of us. And it's important that we remember to look, to look within ourselves to find that echo of kindness, that commitment to community, and that smile that broadcasted respect and humility to this entire city."

Finally, Michael's eye released their lock on the clock in the back of the church. As he scanned the room, he saw the imprint of his mother's impact on each and every person present in the church. A tear escaped from his eye.

"We love you, Mom," he whispered.

THE KID

Ali's bare feet gripped the pavement. His eyes narrowed on his target, squinting to block out the hot afternoon sun. He tightened his leg muscles, readying them for an explosive start. With a glance to his right, and then to his left, he checked his surroundings to ensure an uninterrupted mission.

He looked at his mom for affirmation, which she gave him in the form of a thumbs up. He eyed the water fountain, which spouted geysers all across the plaza. The force of the water was enough to knock him on his butt if he wasn't careful, and the frigid temperature was enough to send him running to the towel his mother was holding for him. He counted the fountain openings: sixteen in all from one side to the next. Ali knew the danger. He knew he had to wait for the perfect moment.

And then it happened; the fountain stopped.

Ali's quads exploded and his feet bounded from their locked position. With toes digging into the cement, Ali sprinted forward. He bounded over one fountain opening. *Safe.* He took two steps and dashed across the second.

As he made his way to the seventh water cannon, the first fountain sprang to life behind him. Ali turned in time to see the second water geyser spout upwards with angry force. The fountains were chasing him, one after the other. His leg muscles worked even harder, pushing themselves to the limit.

Tenth fountain. Eleventh fountain.

Water spewed from the ninth fountain as Ali sprinted over the twelfth.

Thirteenth Fountain. Fourteenth.

Frigid water burst from the fourteenth fountain just as Ali's foot moved out of its blast zone. He sprang across the fifteenth fountain, feeling the force from residual spray.

One more fountain, Ali thought.

He planted both bare feet hard into the concrete and lunged forward.

Splash!

The sixteenth fountain erupted, catching Ali in its frozen wrath. Ali landed on one foot and stood on the cement. He took a deep breath, shivered hyperbolically, and looked across the fountain toward his mother. He locked eyes with her and began laughing hysterically. He sprinted toward her and dove in her direction, where she was waiting with an open towel hug.

"You were so fast, buddy," Mom said.

Ali's face was the only sign of life that emerged from the

towel.

"I almost made it across that time!" he shouted through shivers.

"You sure did," Mom said. "Why don't you dry off, lay on the towel, and let the sun warm you up. Then you can try again soon."

Ali smiled and burrowed further into his towel. His mother opened a picnic basket and removed two peanut butter and jelly sandwiches: one for her and one for Ali.

"And you can eat this while you get warm," Mom said.

Ali laid his towel on the cement and leaned against the bench that his mother was sitting on. He took a bite from his sandwich and watched dozens of other kids dashing through the fountain. Some didn't seem cold, while others conquered their biggest fears by even approaching the fountain itself. Laughing, playful squeals, and parental chatter filled the fountain along the Willamette River's waterfront. The late afternoon sun warmed the air and filled the streets with people who just couldn't stay inside on such a beautiful day.

After a few more sprints through the fountain, a few more comforting runs to Mom, and another snack, Ali and his mother packed up and walked further into downtown, away from the river. They made their way to Pioneer Square, where they saw people leaving work early to enjoy the summer sunshine. They saw people without homes posted up on the steps and curbs, hoping to catch a lucky break. They watched musicians play to crowds that walked by with afternoons coffees. They saw chess players engaged in fierce battles of strategy. And they saw the light rail collect and dispense passengers moving to and from wherever they were going.

As Ali and his mother stepped off the bricks of Pioneer Square, Ali knew exactly where they were headed: the library.

"Mom!" Ali shouted. "Are we going to the library?"

His mother smiled and lifted him up by his arms.

"Yes, we are, my son," Mom said. "You get to pick out two more books today."

"Great!" Ali exclaimed. "Thanks, Mom!"

The entryway to the library gave Ali a sense of wonder and mystery. With its gargantuan columns and elegant staircase, the facade of the library made it look like an ancient palace. Or maybe a temple. One of those buildings Ali had read about in that picture book about Ancient Rome that he checked out last month.

He sprinted up the stairs and waited for his mother at the top. As soon as her foot hit the top step, he opened the heavy double doors and sprinted through them.

"Ali," Mom whisper-shouted, "wait a minute."

"But Mom!" Ali whisper-shouted back. "I want to go find some books."

His mother smiled. Ali's big brown eyes were too sincere. They always had a way of unlocking her attempts at a stern expression.

"Meet me back here on this bench in ten minutes," Mom said. "We'll check out your books after that. Do you understand?"

"Yes, Mom!"

Ali walked briskly toward the back of the library. He wanted to run, but he knew people weren't supposed to run in libraries.

When they came to the library two weeks ago, Ali saw a new book about skyscrapers that he wanted to check out, but he had already checked out two books, so he had to put the skyscraper book back. This time, it was going to be his.

A girl with pigtails emerged from a narrow aisle and cut in front of him. She walked quickly toward the children's section. Knowing that she could be serious competition for the skyscraper book, Ali increased his speed. The girl continued straight into the center of the children's section, so Ali took a sharp left into a secluded aisle. He checked behind him to make sure he was out of the librarian's sight, and then he took off sprinting. When he reached the wall, he planted his left foot and cut hard to the right, sprinting down another aisle. When he reached the aisle with the targeted book, he cut hard and dashed into it, slowing his speed abruptly to hide the fact that he was running in the library.

The girl turned the corner. Ali saw her eyes as they locked onto the skyscraper book, easy to grab, on display under a spotlight. Panic gripped Ali's stomach. Ali and the girl both increased their walking speed, nearly crashing into each other in the center of the aisle. At the same time, they both reached for the same book: an oversized hardcover with a picture of a giant skyscraper.

The girl held tight to the book as Ali also grabbed it. Her face turned down into a pout.

"You can have it," Ali said, releasing his grip.

"Are you sure?" the girl said genuinely.

"Yes, of course," Ali said. "I come here all the time.

Maybe I can get it next week."

The girl's frown turned into a cheesy smile that made her whole face light up.

"Thank you so much!" the girl said. "You're really nice."

The comment and good deed overrode Ali's disappointment. He walked into the center aisle and looked up. A sudden thought overtook his curiosity: he had never been to the second level of the library before.

He turned and found an elegant staircase that took him to the second level. The aisleways edged against a balcony, overlooking the center of the library. He saw his mother reading the newspaper on their meeting bench. Ali wasn't sure if he was allowed to be up here, or if this area was reserved for adults. But the mystery pushed him forward and into a narrow aisle.

All the books in this aisle looked big and boring. For starters, none of them had pictures. And they weren't even about anything cool, like dinosaurs or sailboats. He kept walking, turning right, and then left, and then right. All he wanted was a book with some pictures.

And then he saw it. Posted up on a stand in the middle of an opening, he saw a large, hardcover book with a big picture of a skyscraper. But it wasn't a drawing of a skyscraper like the one he had just sprinted to obtain. It was a real picture. But it was old. There wasn't even any color in the picture. He read the title, and it said something about Portland and its history.

Ali climbed up two shelves and reached as high as he could to grab the book. He clutched it tightly and jumped down to the floor, his footsteps echoing through the empty recesses of the upstairs chambers. He sat against a tall bookshelf and flipped the book open.

Ali saw a picture of a building he recognized, a brick building that featured a rounded doorway and a bunch of people wearing funny hats with huge moustaches; the photograph was taken in 1892. He saw a black and white photograph of his elementary school on the other side of the Willamette River from 1912; all the kids in the picture were blurry and looked like they were moving. He recognized an image of his church from 1925. Then he saw Market Street from 1904, and a small boat on the river from 1887. And a horse-and-carriage from 1884. Broadway in 1936. A theater from 1942. Train yard workers in 1923.

As Ali flipped through this visual history of his city, he had lost track of time. He became immersed in the book itself. And he also didn't see his mother.

She stood in the corner, leaning against a bookshelf, eyeing her son. And then she coughed. One of those audible coughs meant to get someone's attention. And it worked.

Ali snapped his head out of the book and locked eyes with his mother. He had no idea how long she'd been standing here, but he knew he had exceeded his ten-minute time limit. Ali's eyes started to well up. He didn't want to get in trouble. He was just looking for a book.

His mother's expression shifted from stern to adoring. She couldn't remain angry at his curiosity.

"It looks like you've melted into your surroundings, my son," Mom said. "Come on. Grab your book. Let's go home."

She smiled as her son ran into her arms. They held hands as they walked out of the library and back into the city.

The summer sun began to sink behind the clouds. Another day was done, ready to welcome in a fresh start tomorrow with a new sunrise.

THE ROSE

Grandma Rosie walked slowly across the soft green grass in the Rose Garden. She appreciated the smells, the colors, the familiarity. More importantly, she enjoyed watching her granddaughter, Bella, skip through rows of perfectly cultivated roses. She watched as her granddaughter smelled and appreciated the June blooms, the rainbow color palettes. The sun sparkled in her auburn hair.

As her energy began to fade, Grandma Rosie wanted to sit. She found a concrete bench with a panoramic view of the city. Bella poked her head around a row of rose bushes and smiled adorably. She skipped toward Rosie and sat beside her on the bench.

"Grandma," Bella said," I see why you like the Rose Garden so much."

"Oh, you do?" Grandma Rosie said. "And why is that, dear?"

"It's all so pretty," Bella said. "The air smells sweet. The flowers are so colorful. Every rose is different. And I can see the whole city from up here."

Grandma Rosie smiled; her granddaughter was a girl after her own heart. Bella bounded upward and sat on the arm of the bench, facing Grandma Rosie. A serious expression formed on her face.

"Did you come here when you were my age?" Bella asked.

Grandma Rosie smiled; decades of memories flickered.

"Of course I did, dear," she said. "In fact, my parents took me here for the first time when I was ten years old, about your age."

Bella's eyes lit up and an authentic smile graced her face.

"This garden has continued to inspire me as I've grown older," Grandma Rosie continued.

Bella's face wrinkled with a desire to understand.

"What do you mean?" she asked.

"Well," Grandma Rosie said, "a long time ago, it inspired me to write a poem."

"You wrote a poem?" Bella asked. "Can I hear it?"

Grandma Rosie burrowed her chin into her clenched fist. She looked over her shoulder; the city projected a magical backdrop to the sweet smell and vibrant color of the roses.

"Come think of it," Grandma Rosie said, "I've never shared this poem with anyone before."

Bella batted her eyelashes, strengthening the power of her request.

"Since you're my granddaughter, I suppose I'd better pass this poem onto you," Grandma Rosie said. "Are you ready?"

Bella leaned forward, elbows on knees. She gazed directly into Grandma Rosie's eyes. As she spoke, her voice rang out with clear confidence, defined purpose:

A seed is planted in earth,
Soil shaped by aging roses.

The seed sprouts, fighting through the weeds,
Until it breaks free from the ground's captivity.
Sweet sunshine, liberating fresh air;
The rose is grateful for the warmth.

Older roses show the way,
Knowing that growth comes from roots.
Though its stems take sharp turns,
It eventually finds the path to sunlight.

With water and sunlight, the rose blossoms;
Red wings display quiet beauty, sweet scent.

Thorns spring out to fight
Insecure admirers of the rose;
But the rose soars, victorious and elegant.

As spring shifts to summer, the rose feels tired;
From sweltering heat and rough winds,
A petal slowly falls to the earth.

The rose feels pressure to display beauty;

Autumn admirers clamor for its charm.
Seeking solitude, it turns inward,
Wilting as winter wears on.

But, with the first ray of spring sun,
The rose revitalizes, rejuvenates.
Learning from its past season,
And gardeners who cleared a path.

Struggling to find itself again,
The rose recalls its inward motivation:
To fight through the thorns,
To project its beauty to the world.

While surrounding plants flaunt false color,
The rose commands simple allure.
Sun brings new buds, which have
The courage to bloom again.

As the rose grows older, it adapts,
Until it exhausts all its strength.

But the rose's seed is planted in earth;
A new rose begins the journey.

A tear dropped from Grandma Rosie's eye. She watched a red rose blow in the gentle breeze. A pedal fell slowly from its bloom onto the soil. Bella looked intently at her grandmother, waiting to see how she should react.

Growing impatient by the contemplative silence, she jumped up from the concrete armrest and hugged Grandma Rosie. The two stood, held hands, and continued their walk through the roses.

ACKNOWLEDGMENTS

First and foremost, I want to thank my wife and daughter for providing me with positive inspiration, encouragement, and joy throughout the writing process. You've served as soundboards, idea-generators, and reality-checkers. You keep me focused and laughing, driving everything that I do.

I want to thank my parents and siblings for providing me with incredible love and support. You gave me unforgettable experiences growing up in the city of Portland. You introduced me to people from all walks of life, whose experiences have undoubtedly shaped the person I've become.

Additionally, I want to thank my teachers and mentors who have guided me toward becoming a better writer, reader, thinker, and human.

Lastly, I want to thank the city of Portland itself. You gave me a lifetime of memories, experiences, and love. Your history enthralls me. Your contrast bewilders me. Your personality shaped me. And your sights, smells, and sounds formed the basis of my senses. Thank you for all that you have given me and everyone else who has had the privilege to call you "home".

ABOUT THE AUTHOR

Tom Malone was born and raised in Portland, Oregon, where he learned to love rain, coffee, and books. He spent time exploring the city, the forest, and the coast. Malone studied journalism and history at the University of Oregon, Spanish at *la Universidad de Oviedo*, and earned his master's degree from the University of Portland.

He has taken dozens of road trips throughout the United States and continues to travel throughout the world. Currently, Malone teaches secondary English near Denver, Colorado, where he camps, fishes, hikes, and snowboards often.

OTHER WORKS BY AUTHOR

Fiction
Across Americana: A Novel
In the Shadow of the Spanish Sun
Sloan Fitzpatrick: Middle School Journalist

Non-Fiction
World History: A True Story

www.ingramcontent.com/pod-product-compliance
Lightning Source LLC
Chambersburg PA
CBHW020046180626
46812CB00006B/2212